G R JORDAN

The Absent Sculptor

A Highlands and Islands Detective Thrller #37

First published by Carpetless Publishing 2024

First edition

ISBN (print): 978-1-914073-44-1
ISBN (digital): 978-1-915562-99-9

This book was professionally typeset on Reedsy.
Find out more at reedsy.com

The true work of art is but a shadow of the divine perfection.

MICHAELANGELO

Contents

Foreword

The events of this book, while based around real and also fictitious locations around Scotland, are entirely fictional and all characters do not represent any living or deceased person. All companies are fictitious representations. This book was produced from a large block of stone.

Acknowledgments

To Ken, Jean, Colin, Evelyn, John and Rosemary for your work in bringing this novel to completion, your time and effort is deeply appreciated.

Books by G R Jordan

The Highlands and Islands Detective series (Crime)

1. Water's Edge
2. The Bothy
3. The Horror Weekend
4. The Small Ferry
5. Dead at Third Man
6. The Pirate Club
7. A Personal Agenda
8. A Just Punishment
9. The Numerous Deaths of Santa Claus
10. Our Gated Community
11. The Satchel
12. Culhwch Alpha
13. Fair Market Value
14. The Coach Bomber
15. The Culling at Singing Sands
16. Where Justice Fails
17. The Cortado Club
18. Cleared to Die
19. Man Overboard!
20. Antisocial Behaviour
21. Rogues' Gallery
22. The Death of Macleod - Inferno Book 1

The Patrick Smythe Series (Crime)

1. The Disappearance of Russell Hadleigh
2. The Graves of Calgary Bay
3. The Fairy Pools Gathering

Austerley & Kirkgordon Series (Fantasy)

1. Crescendo!
2. The Darkness at Dillingham
3. Dagon's Revenge
4. Ship of Doom

Supernatural and Elder Threat Assessment Agency (SETAA) Series (Fantasy)

1. Scarlett O'Meara: Beastmaster

Island Adventures Series (Cosy Fantasy Adventure)

1. Surface Tensions

Dark Wen Series (Horror Fantasy)

1. The Blasphemous Welcome
2. The Demon's Chalice

Chapter 01

Y ou've got the hands of a god, Ernesto, but you've got the liver of a small child. Get out and get back to your house. You've had enough, okay?'

The tall man came up and hugged him. Ernesto gave a smile. It had been a good evening. It had been a very good evening. Well, what he could remember of the evening was good.

His coat was being given to him and he tried unsuccessfully to put it on. At the third attempt, he simply wrapped it up in his arms, turned, and grinned at his host before stumbling out the door.

It was dark outside. Very dark. What time of the day was it? Up here, in Kylesku, it only got dark in the summer during the true hours of the night. Often, you'd get towards midnight and it would still be at least a twilight, if not indeed be vaguely bright. But this must have been about two in the morning, if not later. He had no watch to validate his assumption. Not much later though, the sun would come back up and he could see again.

Ernesto stumbled forward and then pitched into a run. The slope down from his friend's house was steep, and Ernesto was in no condition to stop his feet from descending rapidly.

At the bottom of the driveway was the road. A single track, but nonetheless, a road. If Ernesto had been in Glasgow or London or somewhere near a big city, he probably would be dead, for a car would have run him over.

Here he stumbled out onto the single-track road, and there was nothing, just a faint breeze in the air. *And something else? Yes, that was it, wasn't it?* he thought to himself. *There's a mild drizzle going on.*

Today had been a pain. The sculpture he had been working on, he had no love for. It was to be done by him. Done simply to appease someone. Done simply to keep his head above water, as they say. Well, he wasn't doing any more of that stuff. He wouldn't be used. He was destined—he said to himself, or possibly even out loud—destined to be up there with the gods. If Zeus himself had been there, Ernesto could have done a sculpture that would have done him justice. Maybe even God himself.

He better be careful, though. Some people around here took offense at such a boast. No disrespect was meant, because, at the end of the day, Ernesto was the best.

He smiled to himself. There was nothing more that he liked, though, than to sculpt Cara. He'd met Cara at an art show and had instantly been taken by her subtle beauty. She hadn't dressed like a model, whether that be classical or outfitted like today's more modern girls. She'd been in jeans, a rather bland rain jacket around her. But the face, oh, the face had been heaven. The jawline, the nose. There was something about her.

It had taken a while to convince her to model for him. She'd been worried at first, for Ernesto's sculptures were usually of nudes, or a little garment thrown here or there. He'd had to be

2

careful in case she thought it was a sexual thing. Well, maybe there was some of that in there, but he didn't want to bed her; he wanted to sculpt her. He wanted to bring her beauty out by creating a masterpiece.

Ernesto stopped and looked left, and then looked right. Where was his house? He stumbled to the left, wandering on down the road where the trees appeared to be dead. The branches seemed to loom. He thought the rain had stopped, but the wind was picking up again. It made little sense, did it?

Rain and wind—they functioned together. The breeze picked up; you got more wind. A front passing through, wasn't that it? Cold, warm? Ernesto didn't know. His was not a scientific mind. His was a mind of greatness. A mind that knew beauty when he saw it and knew how to reveal it to the world.

He stopped for a moment. Off to the left-hand side was the sign that said 'Passing Place'. It was white, a rectangle almost. He looked back up the road behind him and then stared in front of him. His house was before the passing place, wasn't it? It was definitely before. Ernesto turned and pointed himself in what he thought was the right direction back up the road and began stumbling along. It was then he heard it.

In the dead of night, cars on this road could be heard clearly, and Ernesto was standing in the middle of the road. The car was maybe a quarter of a mile away, maybe closer. After all, Ernesto had enough drink in him to impair a superhero.

He thought it best to get off the road and Ernesto stumbled off to the left-hand side. There were trees beyond, but there was a large ditch too. He could take it. The drunken artist swung a leg round and tried to leap off his left foot. Unfortunately, the leap wasn't good enough, and he pitched straight in to the large ditch at the roadside. There was an almost comforting thwack and a splash of water around him. His landing was muddy, but soft.

He heard the car roar past him. Wow, it was certainly close— closer than he had thought. Good job he'd got off the road. He pushed himself up, his hands now caked in mud. Ernesto somehow forced himself back up onto the road. He would change when he was inside. Something like that.

The artist thanked God that he'd left the light on outside his front door; otherwise, he would have walked past his house again. He'd forgotten to look for it the first time. That must have been it.

He stumbled up his driveway, which was also steep until he got to the front door of his small home and studio. He flicked on an interior light, a small one that cast shadows everywhere. Ernesto didn't want bright lights at the moment. Not that he wanted to go to bed. He needed to think; he needed to think about his work and the challenge that had come in recently— the threat that scared him.

There was a loud clatter, and Ernesto looked down to see that he had knocked over a small table. He abandoned it, stumbling off towards his studio. The door was open, and he stumbled in, looking up at the surrounding shelves.

He'd made many of these pieces. Well, he'd made them all, but what he meant was when he made pieces, they came from inside him. Some of these didn't. He reached up and grabbed what was a small horse.

'Utter shite,' he said to himself.

He flung it over his shoulder, hearing it smash behind him. Ernesto moved along to see a bird. This was crap, too. It disappeared over his shoulder as well. As he got to the end of the shelf, he realised the three artworks there were of similar quality. Not something that came from within him. His arm went up, and he went to sweep them off, but missed completely.

He tumbled forward and ended up crashing onto the floor. He felt the wet mud from his trousers stick to it. No point having these on, he thought. Ernesto reached down and fumbled with the laces of one of his boots. And then for the other one. He stopped for a moment. Could he hear something?

He hadn't left the front door open, had he? His mind switched back to the boots. And he undid them, slowly, until at last, he could prise one off, followed by the other. He then took his trousers off, flinging them somewhere in the studio. He sat up, feeling the cold floor through his underpants.

Ernesto was undeterred, and took his jacket off and then removed his shirt. Clambering back to his feet, now only dressed in his underpants, he had another go at the three sculptures on the end of the shelf. He got two of them to tumble off the end and smash on the floor. Ernesto stepped back and yelled before falling over. His foot had come down on top of a piece of cracked sculpture. Maybe he'd cut it. He did not know as he lay looking up at the ceiling.

'I'm ready when you are,' said a voice.

Ernesto fought his way onto his backside, sitting upright, and glanced across at the chaise longue in the corner. Standing beside it was Cara, her long black hair sleeking down over a bare shoulder. She was wrapped in a sheet, covering up her more private areas.

'How would you like me to pose? Classically?' she asked.

Cara doesn't know what 'classically' means, thought Ernesto. *She has no idea. But it doesn't matter. Her beauty is beyond compare.*

She is perfection.

He sat there watching her and then indicated she should take to the chaise longue. She lay down on it, the sheet carefully laid over her, covering her extremities. Even so, she was beautiful.

'How long do you need me today?' she asked him.

'We'll do an hour,' he said. 'Then we'll break, and then we'll do another hour. Then I'll take you for some dinner.'

'We don't do dinner,' said Cara. 'We don't do food. I come in and I model, and you give me money.'

Ernesto stood up, made his way across to his tools, and picked them up. He began to work on a piece of marble. Except there wasn't a piece of marble there. He knew that. It hadn't arrived yet. It was still to be delivered. In fact, had he even ordered it?

He stumbled about in his underpants. Careering back through the house, he found a bottle of wine and looked around for a cork puller. Eventually finding one and after great difficulty with his balance, he came back through with two glasses and a bottle of wine.

Sitting on the floor in his underwear, he poured a glass for Cara and a glass for himself.

'To your beauty,' he said.

Slowly, Ernesto drank, watching Cara on the sofa. He took the glass up, handed it to her, and sat back down again. He thought he'd heard a crash, just after he'd handed the glass over. Continuing to talk to Cara, Ernesto found other voices were getting in the way. Quiet voices, voices from outside, voices he didn't recognise.

'Why would I want to produce any other sculptures when I have you?' said Ernesto. 'There is no point to any of these others.'

'You know you have to do them,' said Cara. She had a very serious look on her face—still quite beautiful, but very serious. Ernesto shook his head.

'I am one of the greats. I don't have to do anything except please my art. It's all your fault,' he said. 'All your fault. There was nothing worth sculpting once I'd seen you. You're the only thing.'

He watched her laugh, a cheeky grin. She wasn't that old. A woman, yes. For Ernesto was a sensible man. He played by the book. If he wanted to sculpt somebody younger, they were accompanied. Or it was done from a photograph. But this vision of perfection was old enough to attend on her own.

There was such a delicate intimacy between Sculptor and those he sculpted. When he worked, they spoke little. But in between times, they would sit and laugh. And drink. This wasn't like a lover—she was much more than that. Ernesto knew they would never be intimate. And yet, the intimacy of the art was everything.

That voice again. Harsh. It was manly, certainly no woman and definitely not the voice of Cara, his angel.

He stood up and turned back to the shelving. He picked up a sculpture which had several fish on it. Well, that wasn't one that was deserved, was it? That one he had not enjoyed. He lobbed it over his shoulder. Goodbye to that one.

It crashed behind him. He heard Cara laugh, giggling. He raced across to another one, yelping as his foot stepped on something. Another sculpture disappeared. Ernesto smiled. *Yes, get rid of it all. Get rid of it all. All of this crap. This utter, utter . . .*

He thought he heard the voice just before he lost it all. A voice that said something like, 'Dear God, he's only in his

7

underpants.' Then there was the thud and a pain at the back of his head. And then there was darkness, total darkness.

Chapter 02

You deserve it. Seriously, have what you want.'

'You should have seen his face,' said Hope McGrath, smiling at her boss, DCI Seoras Macleod. 'I don't think he knew what hit him.'

'Good,' said Macleod. 'That's what you have to do. Keep them on their toes. Don't be predictable. Don't—'

'I'm trying to tell you,' said Hope. 'You said you wanted to know. I've started speaking and you're talking over the top of me.'

'Sorry,' said Macleod. He picked up a cafetiere of black coffee and poured some into a cup.

'I said to him he'd be dead if it hadn't had been for me. They'd all have been dead. I told him if I'd followed his instruction, I'd be alive, but everybody else would be dead.'

'How did he take that?'

'What do you mean, how did he take it?' said Hope. 'What could he do? Seriously, what could he do?'

'You scared me though,' said Macleod.

'Scared you?'

'When you took the dive.'

Hope had dived off the side of a dam with a detonator switch in her hand to keep it away from a bomber. The planted devices would have killed hundreds in the estate far below.

The bomber had set off some smaller explosions in a civic centre, drawing in lots of people. But it was all a ruse to then destroy a dam above the estate and flood the area. The bomber was going to take himself to his own death, except Hope had intervened, having been told to stand down. She'd actually been told to go back to her office and write a report about how she'd failed.

'I hope you didn't back down and let him away with anything,' said Macleod.

'Of course I didn't. I told him, though, that you had trust in me.'

'I had trust,' said Macleod. 'I also trusted you would have got to the guy, instead of having to dive off with a detonator in a seat of the pants' descent into water.'

'Sorry,' said Hope. 'I didn't kind of plan that. It just sort of happened.'

'But you did it,' said Macleod. 'He wasn't so lucky. I get sick of these cases. People getting abused to where they react back so violently. It's not good.'

'Are you tired of it yet, though?' asked Hope.

'I sometimes think,' said Macleod, 'would I be happy if there was no crime, if it was all just peaceful?'

'What would you do with yourself?'

'Well, I'm sure Jane would keep me busy. I think I'd find other mysteries to look into. The world's a mystery; you know that?' said Macleod. 'I haven't travelled enough. Jane likes to sit and enjoy the sun, and that's nice for a while, but I want to find out about things. She's good, though. She'll come with me as long as I sit with her. In some ways, we're not alike. I think that's probably for the best. We'd probably be bored with each other if we were alike.'

'I'm—well, you know what I'm planning,' said Hope, refer-ring to her idea of setting up a family. An idea that was almost scuppered.

'One of my regrets,' said Macleod. 'But I don't think I'd have made a good father.'

'I want to be an excellent mother,' said Hope. 'I'm not sure I can be.'

'You will be,' said Macleod, 'but I am not giving you any more advice. Regarding the job, getting time in the job, how to make space, I'll help, I'll say what I do, but I'm not the best at that. You know that.'

'Maybe Ross will teach me,' smiled Hope. She looked down at the open menu on the table, made her choice, and then passed her order to the waiter who had just arrived. It was a posh hotel, and Macleod had laughed that it was definitely going on expenses.

Hope sat back, coffee in hand and looked across at Macleod. His phone was vibrating. Even Hope could hear it, but Macleod was searching for it, unsure where the sound was coming from. The man was a genius, but the new things in life sometimes taxed him.

'Inside jacket pocket, the one that's hung over your chair,' said Hope.

'Ah,' said Macleod, pulling the phone out and answering it. Hope watched his face. There were several nods which seemed very redundant, considering he was on the phone, until eventually he said, 'Of course, I'll get someone over right away.'

'Something up?'

'The trouble when you run several units is that one thing seems to clash with another. I mean, I haven't even got to sleep since yesterday's bombs, and now we've got a missing sculptor.'

'What?' asked Hope.

'A missing sculptor. Kylesku. Apparently, he's got a studio out there. It's where he lives and he's gone missing. The place has been trashed. They're worried there's foul play in this.'

'You're not racing off to go there, are you?' frowned Hope.

'Of course not,' said Macleod, looking at his phone. 'It's really helpful since I've got the little pictures back. I do like that about these smartphones.'

'The little pictures?' said Hope.

'Yes, I've got it sorted now. There's a separate picture of you all. Ross did it. I press the picture, and you answer. So, this is Clarissa.'

He turned and showed the phone to Hope. The scowl on Clarissa's face in the picture was immense.

'I always like that one,' he said, 'because I know she doesn't want to hear from me. I think she's out with Frank this morning as well. She said something about that. Something like, "Don't disturb me."'

'So why are you disturbing her?'

'If it was a murder, would I ignore you and call Ross?' asked Macleod. 'No, it's your team, and this is her team. If she doesn't want to go, so you can do the spade work and send somebody else. I'm a DCI now, not a DI!' He gave a grin, and pressed the button on his phone.

'Yes, I know you're shopping,' said Macleod suddenly. 'And yes, I know you're with Frank. Yes, yes, you need all the time— just stow it. I've been out all night. I'm having to grab a quick

12

breakfast, and now I'm onto this case. You need to come in and assemble your team. What do you mean, "Who is it?" It's a sculptor in Kylesku.'

Hope laughed, watching as Macleod almost seemed to be badgered by the phone call. He was laughing though, not out loud, for Clarissa would have killed him if she heard him laugh, but his eyes were sparkling. Maybe there was something to this step-up. Maybe he'd begun to learn how to do it, how to be himself in that role. She had to learn that with being a new DI.

Macleod closed down the call. 'We've got about ten minutes before all hell erupts here,' said Macleod.

'I noticed you told her where you were right at the end of the call. You didn't seem to leave a lot of time for her to reply.'

'Are you joking?' said Macleod. 'We're here having breakfast. I told her I was under the cosh. I told her I was coming off a night of not sleeping. She thought I was in the canteen.'

'She will not like this,' said Hope.

'No, and I hope my breakfast gets here before she does. I want to eat some of it in peace.'

Hope reached forward on the table and grabbed a croissant, slicing it and placing some butter inside. As she chewed on it, she sank back into her chair. It was true. Clarissa was a whirlwind, so different to Hope, and yet Macleod liked her— although he was always more uncomfortable in her company than Hope's.

Hope was younger, too. She always thought Macleod looked upon her as his prodigy. Clarissa was never a prodigy. Clarissa was a finished article, albeit a very different one to Hope. A more brutal one, and yet a woman with a great love of the arts.

Hope had never reconciled Clarissa's quite brusque tactics

13

with her incredible passion. Maybe that's just what it was, two sides which had never reconciled. Was she a Lord Byron in disguise? Well, it was a darn good disguise.

Macleod had a piece of black pudding halfway into his mouth when the far side of the restaurant door opened. There were several diners in the room who had been staying in the hotel, having their breakfast. The atmosphere had been quiet and casual.

'I don't care if I haven't got a reservation. Where is he?' said a familiar voice.

'I'm sorry, madam. Who are you referring to?' asked the maître d'.

'Macleod. Where the hell's Macleod?'

'DCI Macleod? Is he expecting you?'

'He damn well is now,' said Clarissa. With a sweeping left hand, she shoved the maître d' to one side, spotting Macleod in the corner. Hope tried not to laugh. The tartan trews were on, the shawl wrapped around her, and the face looked like thunder. Hope was fearing for Seoras's life as she approached. Behind Clarissa, walking serenely and nearly laughing, was Frank, her husband. He was so gentile, a true gentleman. And his eyes were wide as he saw Clarissa approach Macleod.

'Seoras, what the hell? I told you I'm out shopping. I don't get these opportunities. You know I don't take a lot of time off during the day, during the working week. You know that. I was out. Frank was buying me something special. And expensive! I'm in the middle of that and you butt in with this call just because some kid is missing.'

'He is not some missing kid,' said Macleod. 'He's a top sculptor.'

'Who is it?' asked Clarissa.

'Ernesto Hunter.'

'Ernesto Hunter? Seriously? The way you were on about it, I thought it was somebody big. I thought it was somebody with a proper name.'

'He has got a proper name. I mean, he's Italian, and he sculpts,' said Macleod. 'I mean, that fits the bill, doesn't it? All these sculptors are the same.'

Hope put her hand to her mouth. One thing Clarissa didn't like was people talking about art who didn't know about art, and to say that all sculptors were the same . . .

'And that black pudding, that's Stornoway black pudding, is it? Is that from Lewis? Because they're all the same. You understand that? They're all the same, Seoras. You could take any black pudding and shove it in your mouth, and it would be the same.'

Macleod choked on his food and had to raise his napkin as he spat forward, catching a piece. She'd outdone herself this time. She'd hit him right where it hurt.

Macleod had a torturous relationship with the island he was from, but he loved it. One thing he truly loved was the marag dhubh—the black pudding. He had told the team frequently there was no other black pudding like it.

'But we're talking sculptures,' said Macleod.

'Don't! And what the hell's this, anyway? How does she get breakfast? When I cracked my last case, I didn't get breakfast, did I? You didn't wheel me out here. Is it because she's the young one? You know, the better-looking one?'

Hope was nearly in tears with laughter. Clarissa had always shown a slight resentment to Hope. Nothing major, and they'd learnt to work together. But Hope had been her boss, despite having the same rank for a long time, and despite Hope having

15

less experience.

Clarissa had sucked it up, but there had always been an underlying resentment. Hope was also the glamour girl. Those at the top had always seen her as a great media image. Hope understood that was because she was six feet tall and she had striking red hair and a figure. Macleod was unswayed by that and had always held Hope up because of her abilities. The same way as he held Clarissa up, though the abilities were very different.

'Kylesku,' said Macleod. 'The local force there will fill you in further. Apparently, he was out the previous night.'

'What? You've pulled me in because somebody's got pissed and gone missing? Get Mountain Rescue out. Not me!'

'The place was trashed,' said Macleod. 'Sculpture's broken, but only some sculptures. They need an expert.'

Hope grinned again. This was Macleod having had his fun, and now reeling her back in. He was building her up.

'Oh, no you don't,' said Clarissa. 'you are not yet forgiven for that head stunt.'

'Head stunt?' asked Frank.

'The thing I won't tell you about,' said Clarissa.

'She's upset, Frank,' said Macleod, 'because, her boss—and I like to remind everyone here that I am her boss despite the way she's speaking to me—got ahead of one of our killers. A man who wanted to take my head off. I managed to acquire a fake head from some props people. I then enacted the scene that he wanted but used the fake head to make it look as if I'd been decapitated. Trust me, Frank, I was quite touched at the way your wife then looked to beat the absolute living hell out of my supposed killer. I had to stop her.'

'I shouldn't have beaten him. I should have beaten you,' said

Clarissa.

'Clarissa, sort it. Send Sabine. Send Patterson.'

'I can't send Pats,' she said. 'You've been about different sculptures. Pats doesn't know that stuff yet. Pats wouldn't have a clue who our Ernesto Hunter is.'

'Do you?'

'I know his work, maybe not the ins and outs of it. I don't know the traits of everybody's life just because I know their sculptures, just because I've seen their paintings.'

'So, send Sabine,' said Macleod.

'Sabine's in Glasgow. Besides, there's a new guy down. She's breaking him in at the moment. Emmett.'

'Oh yes, Emmett's starting, isn't he? Not sure if he's a fit for the team or not. Good guy, but a bit lost at the moment.'

'So, I get the rejects?' said Clarissa. 'I'm telling you, Seoras, one of these days Hope's going to investigate a murder. And it's going to be darn obvious because there'll be a shawl lying over the body. Your body.' She turned and stormed away. And then halted. 'Are you coming, Frank?'

'Whose car have you got?' asked Macleod suddenly.

'Why?' asked Clarissa.

'We're in hers,' said Frank.

'You don't need Frank, do you?' said Macleod. 'Frank, sit down, have some breakfast. I've never really got to meet you properly. Come on, sit down, and tell me what it's like living with this gem of a woman.'

Frank looked across at Clarissa. 'Have a seat,' she said. 'I'm off to Kylesku. Do make sure you drop him back.' She went to turn away but thought better of it and marched over again to the table.

Standing beside Frank, who was seated and pulling across

17

the breakfast menu, Clarissa leaned down and kissed him on the cheek. 'I'll try not to be long,' she said.

'Do what you do,' he said. 'I'll be here.'

'If there's lobster on that menu, you order it,' she then said to him, before kissing him on the forehead and turning to walk out. She stopped momentarily and looked back. 'I'll swing for you, Macleod. I'm telling you. You'd better pick up Frank's breakfast bill too!' She marched off, out of the restaurant. Hope burst out laughing as soon as she was sure that Clarissa was out of the earshot.

'I'm sure she loves me dearly,' said Macleod.

'No,' said Frank, 'she really doesn't. More of a love-hate relationship, I would say.'

Macleod looked a little stunned and Hope found herself covering her mouth with her hand to stop the well of laughter raging inside her.

Chapter 03

'Full breakfast. I'm telling you, Pats, full breakfast. Croissants, the works, coffee. I'm just surprised there wasn't some champagne there. You believe that? All because she takes a big dive and lands like an Olympic athlete. I mean, that's the thing about Macleod, isn't it? He likes that side of her. Oh yeah, typical man.'

'I've never really found Macleod to—'

'Shut it, Pats,' said Clarissa. 'You're not here to give me your opinion on what I saw. You're here to listen.'

The little green sports car was racing across Scotland, heading for Kylesku, up in the northwest. The scenery was stunning, and Patterson enjoyed that. But his ear was getting bent about the breakfast Macleod and Hope had been having that morning.

'You could have stayed,' said Patterson. 'You could have stayed, and I could have come across. I'm more than capable of looking after a missing person.'

'This is not a missing person,' said Clarissa suddenly. 'You need to understand, Pats, you're on the arts team, yes? Arts team. This is not some humdrum Macleod-murder investigation. This is proper detective work.'

'I don't want to disagree with you,' said Patterson.

'No, you don't,' said Clarissa.

'So maybe I'm not disagreeing; maybe I'm not understanding. How is this "proper detective work" when Hope was dealing with somebody who was about to kill hundreds of people, and risked her own life to stop that from happening?'

'Pats, are you telling me you've been with me this long and you still don't understand the art world?' said Clarissa. 'We're not after a missing person here. This is an absent sculptor. This is someone of importance. And certainly, their work is of importance. He's up and coming. He's not the greatest. But he may reach those heights. His past work seems to be that way, at least what I've seen of it. Are you still getting out to these gallery openings, by the way?'

'Yes,' said Patterson. 'If you remember, I was with you at the last one.'

'Oh, yes, of course you were. You need to be educated more in this wonderful field of ours, but not just educated; you need to have a love for it. You need to develop a—'

'You've told me this repeatedly, as well as telling me I'm a philistine. You said I was worse than Macleod once, when I couldn't identify that painting.'

'Absolutely. The brush strokes were all wrong.'

'Well, forgive me,' said Patterson.

'When we get here, you go in and have a look around the house. I'll get into the studio and have a look at the works, okay? Pick up the basics for me. Let me work on the art,' said Clarissa.

'And how does that help me grow in this art world?'

'Pats, one thing at a time. I told you; we've got a missing sculptor. An absent sculptor. Your development's important, but not as important as the case.'

Patterson rolled his eyes and looked away. He was slowly becoming accustomed to the car. No longer did he put his hand out at every other bend, worried that he might have to brace for impact. But, on the other hand, he was thinking of investing in a beanie hat. Clarissa drove with the top down whenever she could, but often it was freezing. It was no wonder she wore that shawl in the car.

The pair arrived at Kylesku, almost sending a car off to the side ditches as Clarissa raced down the single-track road. When Patterson complained, Clarissa pointed out that she was in fact here on an investigation, and some people needed to learn priorities. She pulled up at the driveway of Ernesto Hunter's house to have a police cordon moved aside for her.

'You see, Pats; that's what hard work gets you. They recognise me instantly.'

And you put the fear of God into them, thought Patterson. When the car pulled up and the pair climbed out, Clarissa was approached by the uniformed sergeant.

'Detective Inspector Urquhart, isn't it? I'm Sergeant McAllister.' The man turned to Patterson.

'DC Eric Patterson. Good to meet you.'

'Well, to be honest, we're a bit lost. We've got forensics coming over to see what they can find, so you'd better suit up before you go in, Inspector. The studio's a mess. There's sculptures here, there, and everywhere. Broken. Looked like they were smashed.'

'Which ones?' asked Clarissa.

The sergeant looked at her. 'I don't know what you mean.'

'Which sculptures are broken?' asked Clarissa.

'The ones on the floor,' said the sergeant.

Clarissa shook her head. 'Right, I'll go in, and I'll have a look. Any idea where he's gone, sergeant?'

'Nothing. We've been next door. Apparently, he was in there for drinks last night. Was pretty smashed when he came out. The guy in there hadn't got a clue when he woke up this morning to a knock from us. He's hungover too. Says he knew Ernesto, though, and they got drunk together, but they were more drinking pals than anything else. He's not of an artistic bent either, so he doesn't understand what Ernesto actually does. I think that attracted Ernesto from what he said, able to just drink with somebody without having them pry into what he did. He was quite a recluse from what we can gather.'

'Lots of artists are recluses,' said Clarissa. 'It's the calm. It's the space to get away. I mean, out here, you're well away from it, aren't you? That's what he's doing. Right, Pats, tie up with the sergeant; see what else you can find in the house. I'm going inside to the studio once I get one of those damn suits on.'

It took Clarissa ten minutes to get herself dressed. She removed the shawl, because under the suit it was just too hot. Soon she arrived at the front door of the house to be greeted by one of the forensic team.

'Inspector,' said the young woman.

'Jona on scene?'

'Not yet. Not sure she's coming out to this one. She's left Derek in charge,' said the forensic officer.

'Oh, aye; not one of Hope's crime scenes, is it?' said Clarissa, leaving a rather bemused woman behind. Clarissa ignored the house, marching through to the studio at the rear. She stopped at the door, looking around. There were indeed many sculptures on the floor.

She looked across at the shelves on the side wall. On the

other side was a workbench, tools, and aprons. There was a chaise longue in the corner with some flowers around it. A place where you could set up a scene. She stopped for a moment, looking around.

It was unusual for a sculptor of Ernesto's level to be throwing the work around and smashing it. Everyone always talked about the artistic temperament. And yes, it was there. She knew that, for she had it. She could blow up with the best of them. But artists had to pay the bills. Ernesto wasn't so great a name that he could afford to just destroy work. The raw material for a sculpture came at a price. Yes, you could make it worth so much more. But there was a cost to stone, a cost to bronze, a cost to all the raw materials.

Why would he smash it? Clarissa bent down and began looking at the pieces.

'Don't move it,' said a voice. 'We're still cataloguing.'

'Don't move it, Inspector!' countered Clarissa.

'Sorry, don't move it, Inspector.' She looked up and saw a middle-aged man dressed in a white coverall. 'I'm Derek. I'm—'

'You're the one they send if it isn't Hope's important cases; is that right?' said Clarissa, leaving the man bemused. 'Sorry,' said Clarissa, 'not your fault. I'll have words with Jona. How are you cataloguing this debris?'

'Well, taking photos of it, lifting it up, putting numbers on each piece along with the photographs.'

'Are you putting it back together?'

'Are you kidding?' said Derek. 'Why would I want them put back together? I mean, it's just smashed sculpture work, isn't it? There's a couple with some blood on them. We're going to have to . . . well, I'm going to analyse that, just in case it's not

23

Ernesto's.'

'What's that over there?' asked Claressa, looking at a pile of clothing.

'That's the clothing he was wearing last night. It's covered in mud. He fell, we think, outside into a ditch, but it's just beyond the house, the wrong side of his house for him coming back. Although they said he was half-canned.'

'Is there any of the clothing missing?'

'Well, there's no underpants. Socks are off, but there's no underpants. Maybe he changed into something else. But there's blood on some of the sculptures. Maybe he walked on them after he broke them. Maybe he walked in and started smashing them up. If he was drunk, he wouldn't have been able to see where he was putting his feet, possibly. I don't know,' said Derek, 'so I'm just cataloguing everything.'

'I want you to do something for me, Derek,' said Clarissa. 'If you'll forgive my earlier rant, I want you to catalogue these pieces, labelling them to say which sculpture they're from, and which pieces we don't know what they belong to. You're going to put the sculptures back together.'

'I am?'

'Yes, you are. And if there's a problem with that, and Jona says it's taking up too much of your time, put Jona on to me. It's a direct instruction. Okay?'

'Okay,' said Derek. 'If that's what you want. But I don't know which sculptures are which. They're all smashed.'

'That's why you're going to get an education today, Derek. You're going to learn about sculptures from the one and only Clarissa Urquhart. And you can call me Clarissa, Derek. You're being most amenable.'

'Okay,' said Derek.

Clarissa stepped forward. 'Have you labelled your pieces yet?'

'Yes,' he said. 'I was just going to bag up.'

'Right then. We'll go round the numbers. I'll tell you which numbers belong with which. And you can put them all together in the same bag, and I'll tell you what bits I'm not recognising. Some of the stuff's so small, I doubt we'll be able to put it back together. But, as long as we get the bulk of it in the right place.'

'Okay,' he said, and walked over to grab a clipboard. He pulled out a pen and began to write. 'You notice I've got numbers beside big bits. We'll make those the main bags. And you can tell me if the small bits fit wherever. Or we'll have a bag that will be just the rest of it.'

'Great,' said Clarissa. 'Tell me when you're ready.' Derek nodded, leaving Clarissa for a moment. She looked along the shelf. There were several sculptures that clearly had the same woman present in them.

'Boss,' said a voice.

'Watch your step when you come in, Pats,' said Clarissa.

Patterson joined her. 'We're into the house,' he said. 'I've got his phone book. He's got his agent, a Sandra Higgs, and other contacts.'

'Sandra Higgs? I know that name,' said Clarissa. 'The thing about agents, Pats, is they don't always know the clients that well. Agents are making money out of them, not making art with them. That woman there is making art with him.'

'What woman?' asked Patterson.

'Pats, look at those sculptures. What do you notice about them?'

'Honestly?'

'Honestly, Pats.'

25

'They must have been done somewhere warm, because she's not wearing many clothes.'

Clarissa rolled her eyes. 'For goodness' sake, this is the art world. It's not Playboy magazine.'

'Well,' said Patterson, 'I can see what his fascination is with her.'

'It's the human body. This would be his muse. He enjoys sculpting his muse.'

'Well, we can see that,' said Patterson.

Clarissa punched him on the arm. 'Wake up. Come on. Art world. Okay.'

'Okay,' said Patterson. 'Well, it's the same woman, isn't it?'

'It's his muse. Sculpting's a deeply personal thing, and a lot of artists, they have this one person. It's like a . . . it's like a . . .'

'Obsession? Some sort of sexual obsession,' said Patterson.

'No! It's seeing the beauty in someone. Clearly he's found her to be good-looking; he's found her to be almost goddess-like. She's basically beauty incarnate; that's what he sees beauty as.'

'Right,' said Patterson, deadpan as ever.

'It's a thing that is very special between Sculptor and Muse. There's nothing dodgy in it.'

'Well, he's got her photographs all over his bedroom,' said Patterson.

'What?' blurted Clarissa.

'He's got photographs in his bedroom, up on the wall. To be fair, she's got a lot less clothing on in the sculptures.'

'What sort of photographs?'

'Ah, just normal ones. She's smiling; she's laughing. Clothed in all of them. I mean, she's not posing in them.'

'We need to find her,' said Clarissa. 'She's not just a muse then. Well, she's really a muse, if truth be told.'

'Well, I'll start having a look. See what we can get on her. What are you doing?'

'Putting the artwork back together. But even from the broken bits, I can tell what's what. Can you tell?' asked Clarissa.

'Well, to a point.'

'What do you mean, to a point?'

'Well, I don't think there's any of her on the floor. None of her sculptures are smashed, are they?'

'Very good, Pats. How do you know that?'

'Well, see that bit over there? I mean, that's a half-naked woman, isn't it?' said Patterson. 'That's not the same as the ones on the shelf.'

'Well, no, it's not. How can you tell?'

'What do you mean, how?' said Patterson.

'How can you tell?'

'She's a little bit size-wise. You know, the boobs?'

Clarissa shook her head. 'It's not even the same type of style,' said Clarissa out loud. 'Pats, for goodness' sake.'

'No, I'm not seeing that,' he said.

'I told Macleod you were a work in progress. I don't think we've even got the chisel out yet. Look, see what comes out of that phone book. See if there's anything else in the house. But we need to find his muse. But we'll start with Sandra Higgs, Okay? What's the address for her?'

'London.'

Clarissa laughed. *Oh yes! Breakfast, was it? Breakfast with Hope? Wait till you see the budget I'm putting together on this investigation?* She smiled to herself, as Patterson shook his head and walked away.

27

Chapter 04

'How on earth could you work in the art world and enjoy working out of that building?' said Clarissa.

'I guess it's modern art, isn't it?' said Patterson.

'No. It's just—it looks horrible. There's no class to it. Give me an old building any day. Have you ever walked through Glasgow? Or any of the other big cities?'

'I walk through them all the time,' said Patterson.

'No, you don't! You just exist through them. You don't walk through them. When you walk, you need to take in your surroundings. And you have to look up. The stonework when you look up, you know, it's amazing, the different details. They blow me away. But I look up at this and I just think that it's just a tall glass. It's just bland,' said Clarissa. 'Come on, we best get it done. Don't show any ignorance when we're in here, okay? Don't talk about the art unless you know it, unless you're sure of it.'

'I never do. I only pitch ideas when you ask me.'

'Good,' said Clarissa. 'That's okay because you're learning from me. Good to know.'

She marched off, Patterson following behind. They rode the lift about halfway up the Shard before coming out and finding the office of Sandra Higgs. It was well appointed and clearly, she was making plenty of money to have an office here. Or was it a status symbol? There was a secretary at the front who took Clarissa and Patterson into a room with a wide view over London. She offered them coffee, but when it came back and Clarissa tasted it, she again gave a shake of her head to Patterson.

'It's one of those pod things. Macleod would never serve you one of those pods. He might pretend he had his head chopped off, but he wouldn't give you coffee like this.'

'This would be seen as posh in London, I would suspect,' said Patterson.

'Well, there you go,' said Clarissa.

They sat for a couple of minutes before a blonde-haired woman entered the room. Clarissa would have guessed she was in her forties, and she certainly used plenty of makeup. Too much makeup. Clarissa was being harsh, but then again, she usually was. The lipstick was red, sharp, too sharp a colour. The foundation was caked on. Clarissa worried the woman might actually crack if she smiled too much.

'Miss Higgs,' said Clarissa. 'I'm DI Clarissa Urquhart. This is DC Eric Patterson. We work on the arts side of Police Scotland and we're currently investigating the disappearance of Ernesto Hunter, one of your clients.'

Sandra sat down suddenly. 'I thank God somebody's on to him. It's been such a worry. I don't know what to do. He's, well, he's just . . .'

'How long have you been his agent?'

'Four years,' said Sandra. 'Four years, and it's been difficult.'

'Why difficult?'

'Ernesto is very unstable. We got him the house out at

Kylesku. He thinks it was for his studio but really we got him away from people. When he went to openings, he never handled people well. Highly strung, but also drinks a lot. Could be off the planet at times.'

'Any drugs?' asked Patterson.

'Occasionally. Not a heavy user. Not an addict, by any means. Wouldn't be averse to take in the odd bit here and there.'

'Has he ever disappeared?'

'He's never disappeared before. His studio was where he lived. His studio was his work.'

'He seemed to be quite fond of a certain model,' said Patterson.

'She wasn't a model,' said Sandra. 'She is his muse. That's what he would refer to her as. His muse. Never said her name. Never told me her name. She threatened to leave him once, and he nearly broke down. I had to come up and stay with him that week. I don't know what it was about, either. What the debate or problem was between the two of them. I don't know who she is; he won't say, but they get like that, you know—scared that somebody else will come in and start using her as a model.'

'When I look at her, she's not got classic Roman features,' said Clarissa. 'She looks quite girl next door.'

'She probably is,' said Sandra, 'but he brings that out so well and translates it into more of a classical style. Whoever she is, she's exquisite.'

'No hints at all where she came from,' asked Patterson.

'I think she's Scottish. But that's it. It's because she liked Irn Bru.'

Patterson nearly burst out laughing, but he controlled himself.

'Is his disappearance a problem to you?' asked Patterson.

'A problem,' said Sandra. 'It's more than a problem. I got some work commissioned for him from an Arab sheik. Five pieces. These guys, they pay over the odds. Don't get me wrong, Ernesto's work is good, and it is getting better, and he's going to be something one day. Really something. And that's what we sell it on to these sheiks for, because they see it as an investment. They don't really have that great an eye.'

'How is he financially off, though?' asked Clarissa.

'Well, the work he gets from me would probably just about be enough, if—well, I don't know his outlays, do I? It would be enough for him to run a studio. But he might have other outlays going on.'

'There were several pieces, different styles, that were smashed on the floor,' said Clarissa. 'I'm trying to get them made back up. I'll send some down to you, see if you recognise any.'

'He only ever did things with his style. It's quite evocative. That's what drew me to him. Because when I met him, I thought he could be hard work. But in this game, that goes with the territory. Oh, the artists are hard work. Especially the geniuses. But he was worth it. He had an individual style, something that said that's him and nobody else.'

'There were different styles in the studio,' said Clarissa.

'He didn't feed any of them through me.'

'Was he selling elsewhere then?' asked Patterson.

'Not under his name. That would be—'

'Insane,' said Clarissa. 'You want to make a name for yourself; you promote your style, Pats. And certainly, Sandra here wouldn't be happy with him diluting that.'

'So, was he moonlighting?' said Sandra.

'All the pieces that were on the shelf weren't just his; there were some others that looked of a different style. But a lot of the ones on the floor—I think all the ones on the floor—were different styles to the one he's using with his muse. I need to speak to her. If she gets in touch, get her to contact me.'

'I doubt she'll contact me,' said Sandra. 'She doesn't even know me.'

Clarissa looked at the woman. Sandra had a smart suit on, trousers. She didn't look like an art lover; she looked like a businesswoman. It laid heavy on Clarissa's heart. She loved her art, but there were plenty of people in it just for the money. Clarissa could buy something for five pounds, and if it had style within it, she would love it as much as a painting she bought for a million.

Not that she could ever get her hands on one costing a million. She'd married a man who cut the lawn at a golf course, and she was a detective. She would need a much bigger budget than what they had.

'Does he have any family?' asked Patterson. 'I got his address book but, there's no family listing in it. It looked like business contacts. Possibly other sculptors. There were some neighbours there, but not many. The local pub, the number for it. It wasn't the most expansive address book I've ever read.'

'He kept himself to himself unless he wanted to drink. He liked Kylesku. I know that. He mentions the locals sometimes.'

'But does he have any family?' repeated Clarissa.

'Oh yes, he does. A sister in Portree, in Skye. She's a painter.'

'Any good?'

'Not at his sort of level. Yes, she can paint. Nice enough but nothing that's going to shake the house. Certainly not worth investing your time or money in.'

Clarissa hated that. Everything was about the pound sign. Not about what was in front of you. Arts for art's sake. If she could teach Pats that, she'd have achieved something.

'You're obviously doing well,' said Clarissa, 'affording this office.'

'Goes with the territory, looks the part. You're talking to an Arab sheik. They want to know that you're somebody with money, you know?'

'Sure they do,' said Clarissa, 'and they'll assume that up here, you've got money. You're not in this building unless you have money.'

'It's quite the icon, isn't it?'

'Well, that's one way to put it,' said Clarissa.

'You don't like it,' said Sandra.

'Ostentatious nonsense,' said Clarissa.

'You live up to your name, don't you?'

So the woman had heard of her. That was good. 'What name's that?'

'The real deal,' said Sandra.

'I like true art. I don't care about the price.'

'I guess that's why you're a detective,' said Sandra. 'Because you know your stuff. You could do what I do.'

'Frankly, you're a mercenary,' said Clarissa. 'Good luck to you, you know. You know your stuff too, to a point. But you've no genuine love for it, do you?'

'Love doesn't buy you a four-bedroom house, doesn't take you on your overseas trips. Love doesn't keep this body looking the way it does.'

No, thought Clarissa. *Love buys you someone who's at home, who's there for you, buys you a friend. Love buys you people who can get you through this life but it also buys you pain.* She held

33

her silence.

'Had he got any exhibitions upcoming?'

'I was waiting for him to finish some more with his muse. Could be a couple of months. I was thinking about opening up a showing with him, but the deal with the Arabs, it was fine. He'd be earning me plenty from that, cover him for the next couple of years and keep him on with me.'

'And you think he will go up to the top?' said Clarissa.

'You've seen some of his work. What do you think?'

'It's good,' said Clarissa, 'it's very good.'

'What about you?' Sandra turned round. 'Detective Constable, wasn't it? What do you think of it?'

'It's not really my thing,' said Patterson. 'But he has a unique style.' He glanced over at Clarissa who was gently nodding.

'He will get there. But he needs an agent to do it. I need to withhold pieces and manipulate the market slightly. Launch him in the correct way. But he'll get there. And he still will do when you find him for me.'

'So, you're sure he's alive?' said Clarissa.

'Well, why wouldn't he be? He's probably gone off wandering. I mean, the only risk is he's got so drunk, he's ended up killing himself walking off a cliff or something. I'm assuming you've had people out looking.'

'We're not sure where to look,' said Clarissa. 'He came back to the house, stripped to his underpants. As far as we know, he may have put clothes on after that and gone somewhere else, but he was extremely drunk when he left his neighbours.'

'Nothing unusual there then,' said Sandra.

'You hear anything, call me,' said Clarissa, taking a card and handing it to Sandra Higgs.

'I will do,' said Sandra. 'It's in my interest for him to be available. It's in my interest for him to do this work. As I said, he'll net me an absolute packet.'

Clarissa shook hands and returned to the lift with Patterson. As they descended in the lift on their own, she asked Patterson, 'What do you make of Miss Higgs?'

'Well, she seems quite genuine. Ernesto is a man on his way up. There could be reasons to make him disappear, but I don't work out how you get money from that.'

'No, I don't either,' said Clarissa. 'Has he gone off on his own? Who knows? His muse was never in any of the deals. We need to talk to her, I think. Sandra Higgs doesn't really know him. We need to find people who know Ernesto though, who know what his problems are, what issues trouble him, or if this is just him charging off.'

'So, we go find the muse?'

'Yes, we do. I'm going to bring Sabine in.'

'To do what?'

'I'm going to put Sabine back up to Kylesku—go round and interview everyone up there. You and I are going to go to visit his sister in Portree to see if we can track down this muse. See if his sister knows anything more about him.

'One other thing, Pats. I liked that personal bit you told her. You didn't put too much forward. All you said was something I'd already told you. Told you about his style. I like that. Never show your ignorance in this world. But don't hedge your bets too much, either.'

'Well, absolutely,' said Patterson. 'If we shift it, we can probably catch the earlier flight back up.'

'We could,' said Clarissa. 'Or we could get some decent food tonight before we get the late-night flight up. Put it on Macleod's budget.'

'Not really necessary, is it?' said Patterson.

'Trust me, Pats. It's very necessary. Breakfast for Hope. He'll pay for that one.'

Chapter 05

Sabine Ferguson sat in the car happily letting the new detective sergeant beside her drive. The tall blonde-haired part Austrian kept casting glances at the smaller individual beside her. DS Emmett Grump was a middle-aged bachelor and was extremely quiet. He'd been quiet since he'd arrived at the Glasgow office to be welcomed by Sabine. Sabine was aware she could cut an imposing figure, for she was tall. She was efficient and certainly knew how to handle herself.

Grump, a mere five-foot-eight, was more squat. With rounded shoulders, he wasn't trim, rather having a slight belly, and his hair was greying. He, however, didn't show any displeasure. He just seemed to be quiet, never engaging the conversation, but replying when asked.

'Have you been up to Kylesku before?'

'No, I haven't, Sabine; it's meant to be quite picturesque.'

'Where do you go on holiday then?'

'I don't, really. I've travelled down to Birmingham a few times.'

Sabine wondered what this meant. Birmingham wasn't a holiday destination, was it? It wasn't like London. London was a holiday destination, albeit a big city. But Birmingham?

Birmingham was, well, a different sort of city.

'What did you do in Birmingham, Emmett?'

'Games convention.'

'A games convention? What, like, videos?'

'No, board games.'

'Board games?' said Sabine, wondering if she was being a little too invasive. 'You mean like Monopoly?'

'No, proper board games. Games that board gamers play,' said Emmett.

'What sort of games are they?'

'Oh, there are loads of different types. And sometimes we partake in roleplay games too. You've probably heard of D&D and stuff like that.'

'Right,' said Sabine. She looked at him. He was in his forties. What was he doing playing board games? Was that a thing? Sabine wasn't a board gamer. Rather, she would be in the gym, if not in an art gallery. Like Clarissa, she shared a love of art but Emmett didn't seem to be that way inclined.

'How did you end up with us?' asked Sabine. 'Not that I'm complaining. I just wondered. Do you like art?'

'Never really thought about it,' said Emmett. 'I'm just waiting to be transferred somewhere else. They're trying to find somewhere appropriate to my skills, they said. It was DCI Macleod. He said that he might have something for me, but not yet.'

'What were you doing before?'

'I had worked on the Glasgow murder squad,' said Emmett, 'but they moved me pretty quick. I was with community services.'

'Did you like that sort of thing?' asked Sabine.

'No,' said Emmett. 'Don't know why they put me there. I

didn't really get on with the murder team. It was a bit . . . well, I wasn't one of the boys.'

'I've never really been one of the boys either,' said Sabine.

Emmett stared at her. 'Well, obviously,' he said. He turned back, focusing on the road again.

'Are you quite happy being with us?' asked Sabine. 'I mean, you've been pretty quiet since you came. You haven't asked a lot. Are you okay working with us? If there are any problems, you can talk to me; you know that.'

'I'm fine,' said Emmett. 'I mean, you're fine, too. Sorry, I'm not a big conversation person. I'm usually quite quiet.'

'That's grand,' said Sabine. 'If you've got any issues about the artwork and stuff, talk to me.'

'I will do,' said Emmett. He turned back. The rest of the drive to Kylesku was in silence, and Sabine, at one point, turned on the radio just to have some noise in the car. Emmett wasn't dislikable. He was just quiet.

They arrived at Kylesku and found the local pub, where Sabine took the landlord to one side.

'You'll obviously be aware that Mr Hunter has disappeared. We heard he was quite a regular in here.'

The landlord was an older man, maybe in his sixties, with a bald head, but a big, toothy grin.

'He was a good customer. Quite energetic with it. Sometimes when he had a bit in him, he would talk and talk and talk. You couldn't shut him up. Not in a nasty way, just all his stories. Often about the art world, or he was into the Greek gods and Roman sculpture and all that. It wasn't really me, but he was harmless. And he was drinking plenty and paying for it. So, I wasn't going to complain.'

'Who did he drink with?'

'Let's see who's in here. That's Jimmy over there. You could talk to Jimmy. Jimmy's in here most of the time. He would have known him. And Ian, or Dixie as we call him. Ian would know. Those two Ernesto talked to more than anybody else. I've seen Ian today. There!'

Sabine and Emmett walked over to sit down beside the men who were sitting next to each other, and Dixie smiled at her.

'I'm DS Sabine Ferguson. This is DS Emmett Grump. We are here to look into the disappearance of Ernesto Hunter. Your landlord says that you guys probably would have talked to him most days, if he was in.'

'Aye,' said Dixie. 'I see most of them that come in. Ernesto talked a lot. Not about anything in particular. Nice lad. Italian, wasn't he behind it all, or at least in the background?'

'Did you notice any changes in him recently? Did he talk about any problems he had?' asked Sabine.

'Yeah, he was a bit—how do I put it—agitated,' said Dixie. 'What would you say?' His head turned to his friend.

'Aye, agitated.'

'He was agitated,' said Dixie.

'What about?' asked Emmett.

'Who knows? He didn't talk about stuff he was having problems with.'

'What did he talk about, though?'

'When he was sober, not a lot. The football. Whatever we were talking about. He just made conversation.'

'What about when he wasn't sober?' asked Sabine.

'Her.'

'Who?'

'Her. The one he used to sculpt. I mean, he was always talking about her.'

40

'Did she have a name?' asked Emmett.

'No,' said Dixie. 'At least none he gave us. It was always her.'

'And she was?' asked Sabine.

'His muse,' said Dixie. 'That's what he called her. The most beautiful woman the world had ever seen and will ever see. Perfection, that was the other word he said.'

'Did any of you ever see her?' asked Emmett.

'He showed us photographs first,' said Dixie. 'And she was lovely, but she was no model. I mean, she looked like a girl next door, but a nice one. No offence, not trying to be sexist,' said Dixie, 'but, you know, there are women next door sometimes and, yeah, you look at them and you think, wow! That was her. But no airs and graces about her.'

'You could tell that from a photograph?' said Emmett.

'She came here once. He brought her in, and she was lovely,' said Dixie. 'Quiet, but lovely. You could see the sculpture in her. You could see the inspiration.'

For a moment, Dixie and his friend seemed to be drifting back to the day.

'Only briefly did they ever hold hands, and it looked very innocent,' said Dixie. 'They never—well, she never looked at him that way.'

'What way?' asked Sabine.

'That way that you women do,' said, Dixie. 'No offence, but, you know, when you like a guy, and especially when you're that young—because she could only have been about—oh, it's hard to say—but you know, you look at each other, don't you? Ernesto was a bit older. But he was like a puppy looking at her, like she was everything. But she never looked that way back. She never gave him that glance that a woman does when she really likes you, in those early days, you know?'

'No, she didn't,' said his friend beside him, 'never.'

'Did she say much when she was here?' asked Sabine.

'Hardly a word. She wasn't standoffish for all that; she didn't ignore us. She was no Madonna, but she was shy, very shy, yet extremely beautiful,' said Dixie.

'What did she look like?' asked Emmett.

'Well, long flowing hair, you know. He has photographs of her. Did you ever see the photograph?'

'Not yet,' said Sabine. 'I'll be going back up to his house to see them soon.'

'Well, you'll see her. The long hair. Stunning. Beautiful hair. Had that sheen.'

'Anything else about her?' asked Emmett.

'Well, I hope this doesn't sound sexist. I mean, she had an impressive figure. Lovely figure. Very curved figure. But what really got you was the face.'

'How would you describe her face?' asked Emmett.

'Enigmatic.' Dixie turned to his friend. 'Wouldn't you say, enigmatic?'

His friend looked back. 'I don't know what that word means.'

'No, you wouldn't,' said Dixie suddenly. 'Her eyes would light up, would draw you in. Her whole face just pulled you towards her. Hard to look away. And yet, it wasn't a face that was saying, look at me. It was just gorgeous. Ernesto said, "Making her eyes come through the sculpture was the hard bit because he didn't have the colour.'

'That's fair enough,' said Sabine. 'I can see that. Do you know what exact age she was?'

'Well, younger than you. Twenty? Twenty-one? Saying that, she could have been thirty. There was a maturity to her as well. But some of the young girls, they have that, don't they?

I mean, we're all different. I wouldn't know what to say you were,' said Dixie, looking at Sabine. Sabine shifted slightly, uncomfortably.

'Oh, I don't mean anything by it,' he said. 'I just mean that you're probably anything between, what, twenty-five and thirty-five?'

Sabine smiled. That wasn't so bad. 'I'm going to get a sketch artist to come over.'

'But you said you had photographs,' said Dixie.

'Sometimes people wear things slightly differently. Their clothes or their hair. Sometimes a sketch picture can help,' said Sabine. 'People have distinct looks, sometimes, when they're in photographs. And some people just do not photograph well.'

'I don't photograph well,' said Emmett. 'Imagine you don't either,' he said to Dixie.

Dixie looked at him. 'That's very forward of you to say so, but very accurate.'

Emmett smiled. He turned to Sabine. 'Do you have anything else, Sabine? I think we should talk to the neighbours.'

Sabine thanked Dixie, and the other man before they left. As they went outside, Sabine nudged Emmett.

'What do you think?'

'I don't know,' said Emmett. 'He's disappeared. Has he gone after her? Well, he doesn't seem to have run. Also, a very bizarre thing to do. Did he come home drunk and then just run out the door? And then everything's smashed.'

'Clarissa said the things that were smashed were not his type of work. Other works.'

'But works he made,' said Emmett.

'Yes, but not all of them.'

'How much effort goes into these sculptures?' asked Emmett.

'I mean, how many hours?'

'Hours,' said Sabine. 'We are talking hours and hours. Amazing amount of time.'

'Even the ones that weren't his style, do you think?'

'Yeah, you can't just knock them out. It's not some sort of factory shop.'

'And yet he smashed them,' said Emmett. 'Why? But not hers.'

'Sometimes it's an artistic temperament,' said Sabine. 'It's not him. It's not what he wants. He's going to smash it.'

'It's not what he wants. Why has he made it?' asked Emmett.

'Well, when I talked to Clarissa,' said Sabine, 'she said that he hadn't been making them for his agent.'

'So who was he making them for? He wouldn't have been making them for himself, would he? You wouldn't make them for yourself and then smash them. Why? If it's not his style, it's not his thing, it's not his muse; dammit, you're making them for someone who wants them. We need to find who he's making them for, or who he made them for.'

'Agreed,' she said. 'Come on, let's get up to his house, see if we can find any answers there.' Sabine drove them up to Ernesto Hunter's house.

There was only a small police presence now since the forensics team had finished. Emmett stopped the car at the bottom of the drive.

'The inspector,' said Emmett, 'in her report ,she said that he had his clothes off. They'd been mucky, and they reckoned he fell. So, he'd walked back past the house and then come back again.'

'Fell over there in the ditch,' said Sabine.

'This is probably spur-of-the-moment stuff then,' said Emmett. 'If he's done a runner, to go after her, he would be all prepared going out into the dark. But he didn't take a car. He wouldn't have caught a bus over the next morning. Well, I assume we've looked at buses.'

'Local uniforms help with that. They couldn't find him travelling.'

'So maybe he's somewhere out there then. In a field.'

'You think that?' asked Sabine.

'No,' said Emmett. 'Why would you wander back out? Why would you come in after falling in a ditch and get rid of your dirty clothes to wander back out? And he smashed all that stuff. He's trollied as well.'

'Trollied?' said Sabine.

'Blitzkrieg. Smashed. Drunk,' said Emmett. 'Something doesn't add up.'

'Did they find anyone else? Any traces?'

'No,' said Sabine.

'Thought there was blood,' said Emmett. 'No blood outside?'

'No,' said Sabine. 'What are you thinking?'

'Oh, he's got blood on crockery inside, on the broken sculpture. If he'd have walked out, that blood would have been on the path coming out. Somebody's taken him out; I'd swear it.'

Sabine smiled. 'Clarissa doesn't like things being sworn to her. Let's go see if we can get some evidence to prove it.'

Chapter 06

'Skye's not been the same since they put that bridge in, Pats. Do you know that?'

Pats suddenly looked around him. He'd nodded off, trying to catch a bit of sleep. It was the morning after London. They'd caught a late flight up, stopped in Glasgow overnight, and then headed out in Clarissa's car. The little green vehicle was whizzing here, there, and everywhere. But Pats had finally become at one with the car and could sleep. To be woken up to such a comment, and clearly expected to provide a response, was just a little too much.

'Well, I'd be fed up waiting if I had to get a ferry over.'

'It's part of the song, Pats, you know. People don't appreciate old things; they don't appreciate the way things were. Nowadays, people bomb into Skye in their cars.'

Patterson looked around him, seeing the greenery race past the car. If anyone was bombing into Skye, it was Clarissa.

'And that's a bad thing,' said Patterson.

'Do you know how much this place gets swollen in the summer? How many more tourists? I mean, I can't imagine living here. And the roads, they're not designed for that volume of traffic. I mean, there's nothing wrong with the roads; they're

46

just not big enough. Can't do much about that. Can't suddenly back-lay all these roads for a massive increase in traffic.'

'I guess not,' said Pats. 'Whereabouts are we going again on Skye, anyway.'

'Portree. Near to the harbour. I've got the address and we've got the map on the phone.'

'So, I'm okay to go back to sleep until we get there?' asked Patterson

'No, you are not. Your boss is talking to you. Pay attention.'

'Same way as you pay attention when Macleod talks.'

'You stop that. You stop that right now, Pats. Okay? You don't talk about Macleod like that.'

'You talk about him like that,' said Patterson.

'Yes. Well, I'm allowed to. You're not.'

Patterson rolled his eyes and lay back in the seat. He felt an elbow nudging him. 'So come on, you can start talking to me about famous painters.'

'No, I can't. It's too early in the morning,' said Patterson.

'Right then—you can listen to me.'

For the next hour, Patterson did his best to ignore Clarissa, wittering on about various painters. She knew all their histories in depth. She talked about unique pictures, describing each one. Talked about the fakes that had emerged around them. She was a walking encyclopaedia of the art industry. Or so it seemed to Patterson. And she didn't seem to take a breath as she spoke.

This, of course, was all done as the car sped round the roads. Yet she looked like she was sitting in a comfortable chair, with a brandy at her side, just chewing the fat. *Some woman*, thought Patterson.

When they arrived in Portree, Clarissa found the house of

Esme Silverstone, Ernesto Hunter's sister. The house was a tiny cottage, quaint enough, if you like that sort of thing. Clarissa, in her shawl, and Patterson, with his cravat, marched up to the front door, looking like they were professionals from the Antiques Roadshow.

Clarissa banged on the door in that gentle manner she believed she had—brutal delicacy, as Patterson would have put it. The door opened and a petite woman with white hair tied up in a bun, stood looking at them. She couldn't have been that old—forty, maybe?

'I'm DI Clarissa Urquhart. This is DC Eric Patterson. We're here to ask you some questions about your brother and his disappearance.'

The door went to shut. Clarissa slammed her foot in it, but the door was hit with such force that it made her give a yelp.

'If I may,' said Patterson, and he put out his left hand, keeping the door open. 'We need to talk to you about your brother, Ernesto. Are you Esme Silverstone?' asked Patterson.

'Yes, but he'll turn up. He'll be fine. Don't worry. He'll turn up.'

'I'm afraid that's not good enough. You see, we have to find him,' said Patterson. Clarissa, at this point, had taken her foot away from the door and was rolling it around her ankle, trying to get some feeling back beyond pain.

'Can you open the door and we'll come in and talk?' said Clarissa.

'No, don't come in,' said Esme. 'I don't want you to come in. I don't know where he is. He's gone. He does this. He'll disappear. He'll come back.'

'No one up on Kylesku said that,' offered Clarissa.

'Well, they don't know him like me. He's got a wandering

soul. Go away. I don't need to talk to you.'

'We may come back,' said Patterson, 'if enquiries indicate we need to. It would be better if you were more open with us.'

'No,' said Esme, and shut the door. Patterson looked at Clarissa, but she gave a flick of her head, showing they should return to the car.

As they drove away, Clarissa turned to Patterson. 'What do you make of that, Pats?'

'We keep an eye,' said Patterson.

'Good idea,' said Clarissa. 'Get out. I'm going off to phone Macleod. Tell him what's going on. See what Sabine knows too.'

'I could drop you somewhere,' said Patterson. 'I could take the car back then.'

'It's a little green sports car, Pats. She's just seen it outside the house. How are you going to hide in my baby?'

'That's why I said we should bring mine,' said Patterson.

'Pats, this is the art team. We do things with a touch of class. I am not driving a Fiesta.'

Patterson shook his head as he got out of the car. Clarissa then went to pull off, but he banged the side of the car twice.

'What, Pats?'

'I'm just going to get my coat.' He lifted his rain jacket out, and hadn't even got it on by the time Clarissa had spread away. Patterson dressed in his coat and then wandered back towards the house.

Clarissa was . . . different to work with. That's how you would put it, wasn't it? She was all drama. But she'd saved his life. And she knew her stuff when it came to the art world.

The art world was not the world of the Murder Squad. It was different. Or so he kept telling himself. So far, he'd seen somebody get their head blown off in front of him. That sounded more like the Murder Squad. Except with the Murder Squad, you usually ended up finding that out later.

His hand reached up under the cravat and traced a line on his neck where he'd had his throat slit while on the murder squad. Clarissa had saved him and whenever anybody talked about the way she was, he always related the story, always told them. She had kept going, hanging on to his throat, keeping him alive.

He would be eternally grateful, and putting up with her eccentricities wasn't much. After all, she'd also found him a home. That was her doing, not Macleod's. She had brought him under her wing. He knew nothing about art. He often felt out of his depth, especially with Sabine. Just like Clarissa, she knew her stuff.

Patterson walked out towards the cottage and found a bench a little way down from it. He sat there, pulled out his phone and read a book on it. Patterson was reading a discourse on several artworks. He might as well catch up while he was on company time, so to speak. But as he did so, he saw a man in a suit arrive at the house.

He'd walked from the opposite end from where Patterson was sitting. And now he was approaching the door of the house. Patterson put his phone back in his pocket and walked towards the house.

The front door of the house opened, and he glimpsed Esme's face as she looked at the man. She seemed shocked, afraid even, and Patterson wondered what was going on. The man was quickly taken inside and Patterson turned down the short driveway, making his way quickly round to the rear of the house. He saddled up close to the kitchen, where he could hear some raised voices.

A raised voice said, 'You know what will happen, don't you!'

He could hear Esme crying now, and he wondered if he heard a slap. Patterson pondered about whether he should step in, question the man to find out who he was. But it was sometimes better to observe. He had heard no noise that said that Esme was in complete danger, that she was going to be seriously attacked or have her life threatened. So instead, he held back, texting Clarissa. Before he could get a reply, the man was back out of the house and walking away.

Patterson stayed close behind, a reasonable distance away, but close enough that he wouldn't lose the man. The man walked approximately one hundred and fifty metres before a car pulled up and he climbed inside. As the car drove away, around the corner, Patterson heard a car behind him. He stepped out into the road, holding up his hands and reached inside for his warrant card. It was then he saw the L-plates. A learner driver with an instructor inside.

Patterson opened the rear car door and climbed into it. 'Sorry to bother you. DC Eric Patterson. I need you to give me a lift and follow a potential criminal. Carry on down the road.'

The instructor turned and advised this young student to continue. Patterson could see the tension in the front seats, but when they came round the corner, he saw the car up ahead. They followed it along several roads before the car stopped. When Patterson advised the learner driver to continue on past, and when she had done so by a significant distance, he asked her to stop and got out, thanking them both. Patterson walked back towards the car they had followed. Around it were several gentlemen in suits.

Patterson got his phone and pulled out some earphones. He put them in and held his phone out in front of him as he walked past the men. As he did so, instead of having music on his phone, he had his camera up, snapping several shots as he walked past, pretending he was adjusting the tracks on his music.

When he got to the other side, he hid round the corner, peering back to see the men disappear inside a restaurant. He texted Clarissa to say where he was, and then stood outside, watching. He took a photograph of the car number plate, until eventually he saw a small green sports car approaching. She didn't stop outside the restaurant, but carried on past and caught Patterson's signal to turn down a side street. When he got there, Clarissa seemed quite buoyant.

'She was threatened by one of these guys in the restaurant. Don't know who they are, but I got some photographs,' said Patterson.

'Well, we need to send them off then, don't we?' she said. 'In the meantime, we'll keep an eye on the restaurant.'

Patterson also made a call to the local police, asking that they keep dropping by Esme Silverstone's house. Just a passing patrol to make sure no one was there, but if so, to stay close.

It was several hours before the men came back out of the restaurant. They got into different cars, disappearing off. Patterson asked Clarissa what they should do.

'They're all heading off different directions, and we've no idea who's who. But we know this restaurant. We know they want Esme and you've got photographs. I say you've done a good job, Pats. First thing we do is find out who these people are. My money is, somebody will clock them, and they'll know who they are. You don't threaten people like that, not so smoothly, without being someone. And then they went and had lunch. Smacks of the criminal underworld. I think it's time we called the team in and had a proper talk. In the meantime, let's find somewhere to sleep tonight.'

As Patterson went to search for somewhere on his phone, she tapped him on the shoulder. 'And remember, somewhere posh, Macleod's paying.'

Chapter 07

'Hello, Emmett, I'm your new boss,' said Clarissa. 'Sorry I haven't met you yet. I was coming down to see you until Seoras here sent us out to Kylesku. He was too busy having breakfast.'

Patterson, standing behind Clarissa, shook his head on the screen, wondering what Macleod would make of that.

'I can't believe that a little breakfast gets you this jealous. Frank must have told you how good it was,' said Macleod. Clarissa scowled at him.

'Anyway,' said Clarissa, 'that's not what we're here for. Did we get anywhere with the photos that Patterson sent in?'

Macleod, on the other end of the call, started pressing things on his laptop.

'They're not coming up,' he said.

'Well, we can't do anything about that,' said Clarissa. 'We're on the other side of the call.'

'I know that,' said Macleod. On Clarissa's screen, there was a little box showing Macleod, and another small screen showing Sabine and Emmett. Everyone temporarily looked the other way, while Macleod looked over his shoulder.

'Ross in? You think Ross could do this?'

Soon, Perry appeared over Macleod's shoulder. 'You just press that there, Seoras. That one. No. Do you need me to stay?'

'No, I don't,' said Macleod. 'Go on. Thank you.'

As he turned back to face the screen, Clarissa was smirking.

'Well, this'll wipe the smirk off your face,' said Macleod. 'One of the men in the photographs is Dexter MacPhail.'

'And I should know him?' asked Clarissa.

'Possibly. He's one of Glasgow's biggest crime bosses.'

'That he is,' said Patterson. 'You know him well, Seoras?'

'I do now. Do you recognise him, Patterson?'

'I wondered about that face, but I only saw him briefly, so I didn't want to say. Better to get the proper confirmation.'

'Pats, you say whatever, and you say it however likely it is. You don't just say nothing. How bad's this Dexter MacPhail?' asked Clarissa.

'Oh, he's bad. He's definitely bad news,' said Macleod. 'This is a guy that puts people in the ground. I've clashed with him a few times when I was down in Glasgow. It's been a few years now though, but I don't think he's got any happier in his old age.'

'I'm sure he'd say the same about you,' said Clarissa. The eyes of the others on the screen momentarily averted.

'Seriously,' said Macleod. 'Be very careful. He's not behind the door in just disposing of someone. He'll understand how to do it. So, when you investigate, be very careful. No unnecessary risks.'

'When do I ever take unnecessary risks?' said Clarissa.

'Subtlety,' said Macleod. 'Keep it subtle. That's what you need. Okay?'

'I hear you, boss,' said Clarissa. 'But, the question remains, what is he doing here? Why have we got a Glasgow crime boss in Portree?'

'He wasn't the one doing the talking,' said Patterson. 'The guy that went in—who was he?'

'The other ones are cronies. They're all just his men,' said Macleod. 'None of them are high up. But if he's talking to Ernesto's sister, and Ernesto is missing, he's either looking for him, or he's the reason he's disappeared.'

'Might it be drugs then?' asked Sabine. 'I know Dexter MacPhail's heavily into drugs.'

'How do you know that?' said Clarissa.

'Because I'm in the Glasgow office,' said Sabine. 'I do talk to my colleagues in the other departments.'

'Did you know him, Emmett?' asked Clarissa.

'No,' said Emmett. 'I don't hail from Glasgow. I haven't worked there long either. MacPhail's name never came up in one of my investigations.'

'Good,' said Clarissa. 'That gives me an idea, but I don't think it's drugs.'

'Well, Hunter definitely took them, didn't he?' said Sabine. 'It'd be an obvious thing. Maybe he's making stuff for other people because he owes them money for drugs.'

'He broke them all, though. Why would you? Just pay them off with them, if that was the reason he was doing it,' said Clarissa. 'But this guy could have made money back in no time. I mean, would MacPhail not be wise enough to realise this is a star on the up?'

'How guaranteed is that?' asked Macleod.

'Well, if Sandra Higgs in charge of him, it's highly likely. I mean his work's superb. He'll be making a pretty packet soon,' said Clarissa.

'And what about the drugs before then?' said Macleod. 'The debts keep spiralling. These dealers have a level and then they stop, and they call it in. They don't keep going and going because they realise when somebody's not going to be able to pay it all. They'd rather have their money than put somebody in the ground. These are business people.'

'I know that, Seoras, but the fact remains he could have been worth a lot to them, much more than a simple drug debt.'

'We're operating with no concrete evidence. We need to keep an eye on them, I would suggest,' said Emmett.

'I agree,' said Clarissa, 'and I think Sabine and Emmett should do it. Emmett because they won't know him, and Sabine because she understands Glasgow. Pats and I would be out of our area. I could do it, but Sabine is the ideal person.'

'I think you're right,' said Macleod. 'You happy with that, Sabine? Emmett, you take your lead from her?'

'Not a problem,' said Sabine. 'We'll call if we need help.'

'So, what are you going to do?' Macleod said to Clarissa.

'Well, Sabine and Emmett will search around Glasgow. We know his muse went to Kylesku. We've got a good idea what she looks like, but we've got no names. From his house, we've still got the rest of his address book to go through. So far, that's dug us up one contact, his agent. She's a dead end. So let's go through the rest of the book. See what we can come up with.'

'Nothing more inspired? Nothing in the art world you could go to?' asked Macleod.

'He's quite a private person, from what we gathered. Sandra Higgs was a good contact into the world. He's dealing with her to get his stuff out. That's the way a lot of these people work. Artists are not like you,' Clarissa said to Macleod. 'They're not all showy with their big breakfasts. Instead, they like to be out of the way. They just want the art.'

'So how many names does he have in his address book then? And do you think they're what, friends? Family?'

'I think one will be his muse,' said Clarissa. 'We don't know her name, but we have a photo and sketch artist's impressions from the men in the pub. I think we find his muse and she'll know everything. These guys, well, they worship these models.'

'Just because they're good looking?'

'You don't get it, Seoras,' said Clarissa. 'It's not like that. It's not a purely sexual thing. They are the embodiment of their art, what they want to reproduce because they see them as perfect in form. Not someone they want to go out with. They're way beyond that.'

'I think you're right, Clarissa,' said Macleod. 'I won't understand it.'

'She's right though, Seoras,' said Sabine. 'And he probably talked to her about everything. When he was in the pub, he didn't tell them anything of substance. When she came into the pub, they didn't even get her name. That's his confidant. That's his all-in-all. Whether or not she believes she is may be another matter. Maybe she's just making money. But she also doesn't live local because they would have known her. I think Clarissa's right. Search the address book. Find her and you might find more of the story.'

'Okay,' said Macleod. 'I'm still stuck up here, so let me know how it goes?'

'What's it tonight?' said Clarissa. 'Dinner for two?'

'You can stop that,' said Macleod. 'When you dive in to save lives, into a tiny fraction of water, I'll happily take you for breakfast.'

'I pulled you away from a cult,' said Clarissa. 'You owe me more than breakfast.'

'Probably,' said Macleod. And then with a wry smile he said, 'but Hope did it with such style.'

The screen was gone before Clarissa could react. Her face was raging, but she pulled it back and gave a wry smile as well.

'Our beloved Detective Chief Inspector is gone. Right, Sabine,' said Clarissa. 'Be careful. No risks, from a distance, everything. Okay? Don't be afraid to keep a few things on you, if you know what I mean.'

'You're the one that needs to keep things on you,' said Sabine. 'I can handle myself.'

'Make sure Emmett knows, too. Emmett, we'll get together at some point, because I'll need to talk to you. Do you know much about the art world?'

'It'll be a quick conversation,' said Emmett.

'That's fine. You can learn like Pats does.'

'He likes board games,' said Sabine.

'What, like Monopoly?' said Clarissa. She saw Emmett roll his eyes.

'No,' he said. 'Proper board games.'

Clarissa didn't take it any further. Board games weren't really her thing.

'Nice to meet you, though,' said Patterson and Emmett gave him a nod. Clarissa closed down the call before closing her laptop. She turned to Patterson.

'Why is Ernesto involved with these gangsters?'

'Sabine could be right. Could be drug related. It could be—'

'No, it's not,' said Clarissa. 'The other thing is, they obviously don't know where he is, because he'd be dead. Or, they'd have roughed him up to get their money, or whatever else they want him to do. And he's also vanished. Gone, gone. It doesn't make sense. I wonder if MacPhail's grabbed him.'

'Well, he's got the form for it,' said Patterson. 'We know that for sure.'

'Off you go to bed,' say Clarissa, 'or whatever you want to do. I'll see you in the morning and we'll start trawling the addresses.'

'Do you want me to plan them out tonight, get a route together?'

'See what you think. See what you think are the best options. Remember, we're looking for women.'

'Absolutely,' said Patterson. 'All I've got to do is find the most beautiful woman in the world. Shouldn't be that difficult.'

Clarissa laughed. She watched Patterson leave before she picked up her phone and called Frank.

'How are you, love?' he asked.

'Taking on a bit more than I wanted,' she said. 'I'll be down, well, part of my team will be in Glasgow. I think I'm heading elsewhere tomorrow. We've got to track down the most beautiful woman in the world.'

'But that's easy,' said Frank.

'Don't,' said Clarissa. 'Just don't. That's too cheesy.'

'Shot a seventy-eight today,' said Frank.

'Did you use a buggy?'

'No, I didn't use a buggy. I walked round the course,' said Frank.

'Damn it, Frank. I told you to use the buggy.'

'No need for a buggy unless you're there,' said Frank. 'I'm perfectly capable of walking round.'

'You had that twinge though, didn't you? Don't man up just

because I'm not there. Just because you can't turn round and say, "Oh, Clarissa's using the buggy," which is not the reason that we go in it.'

'You know,' said Frank, 'sometimes I miss you. And sometimes you just give me an earache.'

'But it's a loving earache,' said Clarissa. She went quiet for a moment on the phone.

'How's Patterson?' asked Frank.

'Pats is doing well. Good partner. Got a new guy in, Emmett. Likes board games. Not sure how he's going to turn out. Macleod got him in. Not sure I trust Seoras anymore.'

Frank laughed. 'Of course you do.'

'Did you have the lobster for your breakfast?'

'I didn't do lobster for breakfast, but it was very enjoyable,' said Frank. 'We should go there at some point.'

'No, we are not going there. If we go there, Seoras will take me there. Seoras owes me this.'

'You need to get over this with him. You know he's winding you up.'

'Of course I know,' said Clarissa. 'I don't think he knows what he did that day. He's able to just shrug things off. People don't see that about him. He's able to cope with the rough, take things as they are, move on. Not me. That's why I didn't like the Murder Squad. I wasn't so good at that.'

'No, you're not. But that's why you have me,' said Frank.

'That's it,' said Clarissa. 'Absolutely.'

'What are you going to do now?' asked Frank.

'Cup of coffee, go to bed,' she said. 'I'm exhausted. I don't think Pats sees that.'

'More like you don't show it.'

'I don't, Frank. Why am I still doing this? Why am I still

chasing round the country in a little green sports car?'

'You love that car, don't you?'

'I do, Frank. I want you sat beside me, though, however much that terrifies you.'

Frank laughed at the end of the phone. 'You can stop any time you want.'

'I know,' she said, 'but I guess I'm enjoying this now. The art, I mean. Today I was good. I know what I'm talking about and find this world easy. I brought things about those sculptures to the party before anyone else. I'm at home here. And I'm running my team. I never got the chance to run my team before. They always said I was too bullying, too strong. Never played by the rules. As much as I want to kill Seoras, he gave me this team.'

'Yes, he did. And he actually brought us together. If you hadn't been on the murder squad, you never would have been at the golf club,' said Frank. 'So maybe you owe him breakfast.'

'Frank, if you ever say that to me again, you might find that our marriage is a short one.'

Frank laughed. She spoke for another hour to Frank, letting go of the troubles of the day. Frank had been good for her. She wondered how she ever managed without him now.

Chapter 08

Sabine marched into the Glasgow station, feeling comfortably at home. This had been where the arts team had worked from for a while now. And she was becoming part of the place. It was hard to miss the big, half Austrian, half Irish woman, at six feet and blonde. She struck an image. One that must have seemed strange now, that the more diminutive Emmett was walking behind her.

He had this thing where he never took the lead. He followed, and very quietly. Fair enough, he was going into a station where he knew next to nobody. But he didn't seem to be keen to stamp his presence anywhere.'

'We'll talk to some of the guys who deal with the organised crime. Jim McIntyre is one of them. I'll warn you; he likes me.'

'In what way?' asked Emmett.

'He has a few pet names for me. I play up to him a bit. Get something out of him. I've put him in his place before though. He's okay.'

They turned round the corridor and Sabine opened an office door. As she walked in, a cry came from the back of the room.

'Hey gorgeous, what about you?'

'Are you wise, wee man?' said Sabine, putting on her thickest

Northern Irish accent. She muted it at times, but with Jim, she was quite happy to let him know where he stood.

'Got a sidekick with you now. Some guys get all the luck.'

Emmett looked across at him and gave his head a shake.

'I'm afraid Emmett's into a bit more than just girly mags like yourself, Jim.'

'Don't knock them. I've told you that you can come and have a look at mine any time you want.'

'More like you want me to be in them,' said Sabine. 'You're a dirty old man.'

'I've told you, I don't have Hugh Hefner's number anymore.'

Sabine walked over and clipped him round the ear. 'That's enough of that. You can get kicked out of the force for that these days.'

'Not from you though,' he smiled.

'Jim,' said Sabine, becoming more serious. 'MacPhail, Dexter MacPhail, what's he been up to?'

'Dexter MacPhail? What's Dexter MacPhail not been up to? Dexter MacPhail is always up to something, and it's usually not good, but you're the arts team. Why are you talking to me about Dexter MacPhail?'

'Dexter MacPhail, or at least one of his associates, was seen threatening a woman in Portree.'

'Portree?'

'Has it not come through yet on the shared info route?' asked Sabine. 'Macleod identified him from the photographs.'

Jim sat up. 'Macleod's involved?'

'Just at the top. My boss, Clarissa Urquhart, has got me wanting to look at MacPhail.'

'Urquhart? You're really dumping me in it, aren't you, Sabine? I'm delighted to see you, but trust me, don't bring me traffic like this.'

'Do you know anything about him—about Portree?' asked Emmett.

'I don't think we've been introduced,' said Jim.

'DS Emmett Grump. Do you know why he would be in Portree?'

'Grump? Well, at least you live up to your name.'

Emmett sighed. 'You're not the first,' he said. 'Do you know anything about him?'

'You're a lot more fun, Sabine. I have to be honest.'

'I don't think Emmett's got the correct parts for you to be interested, Jim,' said Sabine, sitting down on the corner of Jim's desk, 'but he's asking the right questions.'

'Know nothing about it. No contacts out there as far as I'm aware.'

'Also, he was threatening someone,' said Emmett.

'Who?'

'The sister of Ernesto Hunter.'

'Who the hell is Ernesto Hunter?' asked Jim.

'Would you pull your computer up? Look at your emails.'

Jim clicked on his screen and pulled his emails up. 'Oh,' he said. 'I thought that was just—'

'You thought it was what?'

'Macleod and some of these other ones, they get them to put stupid faff up nowadays. Police like this, say the right thing. They have to put them out. I thought . . .'

'You better have read this. If Macleod finds out you haven't read it,' said Sabine.

'Of course.' Jim clicked on the email and started scanning down. 'Oh hell, he wanted a reply as well.'

'As do I and as does my friend here, DS Grump.'

'We don't know anything about him being out there. Those other clowns, they're his cohorts. They're just doing his work for him. You say this guy's a sculptor?'

'Yes, up and coming one,' said Sabine.

'I have no idea what the hell MacPhail wants with him. You know? No connections in Skye. Give me a minute.' He clicked on his computer elsewhere and then brought up an image of a woman.

'This woman here is Janice Stewart. Nice piece of work like yourself.'

Sabine ignored the comment, staring at her. 'Who is this?' she asked.

'That's his latest fancy woman. She runs one of those art studio type places.'

'Why do I not know Janice Stewart?'

'I don't know. She's in the art world.'

'I can name you all the art studios in Glasgow. That's not one,' said Sabine.

'Well, maybe she's only just got going.'

'She's not dealing on the normal circuit,' said Sabine.

Emmett peered over her shoulder, staring at the woman. 'Have you had any dealings with her?' asked Emmett.

'Well, she's a lot younger than him and to be honest, I think she's just a bit of skirt for him.'

'Who uses words like "a bit of skirt for him" anymore?' said Sabine. 'You are a dinosaur.'

'Good-looking dinosaur though, eh?' said Jim. He gave her a push playing with her. He was lucky, though, that it was a push on the hips. If he had been any cheekier, she'd have slapped him. Jim was a relic from an old age and yes, he would do these things. This playful, flirtatious banter that they were told had no place anymore. But Sabine let him, because he fed her titbits. He fed her the information that wasn't always meant to be fed across.

'You've looked into her, then?' asked Sabine.

'Well, yes, we've looked into her,' said Jim.

'Did you personally look into her?' asked Emmett.

Sabine burst out laughing. 'Oh, you bet. A face like that—Jim has looked into her personally.'

'Now, now, in my professional duty. I was actually on a stakeout watching her for several nights. We also investigated her establishment for money laundering, but couldn't find anything to generate further investigations. She's just his bit on the side.'

'She's got quite a resemblance,' said Emmett, 'to Hunter's muse.'

'Hunter's what?' asked Jim.

'His muse,' said Sabine. 'Bit like I am to you, only more sordid between you and me.'

'What the hell are you talking about?' said Jim.

'His muse. A muse is the one that the sculptor always replicates, the beauty he always wants to portray in his sculpture. So Hunter's Muse would have posed for him.'

'Like proper sculpting,' said Jim, 'the one with the clothes off and stuff.'

'Seriously,' said Sabine, 'these are classical pieces; these are—'

'Oh, you're not getting me with that,' said Jim.

'No, I wouldn't have thought so,' said Emmett suddenly.

Jim stared at him. 'She's able to take the mick because I know her. Now, you—'

'She looks a bit like her. But it's not her, she's too old. But it might be . . . it'd be a way for MacPhail to have got started on art pieces,' said Emmett.

Sabine turned and stared at Emmett. 'How do you mean?'

'If MacPhail has got anything to do with Hunter, he had to come across him. From what Jim says, he's not an art man. But maybe he saw the pieces at some point. Maybe that's what drew him in, if this is the type of woman he likes.'

'That's very good, Emmett,' said Sabine.

'Is she your sort of woman, then?' asked Jim. 'What does Sabine think?'

'I'll have less of that,' said Emmett. 'Damn it. I work with Sabine. She's been nothing but courteous. The fact that she looks like she looks is neither here nor there. I really don't like the way you're talking to her.'

'Look, you've just walked in here, and—'

'Easy, boys,' said Sabine. 'Easy. Same team here. Okay? So, what do we know? She looks a bit like Hunter's muse. We know MacPhail has her as a girlfriend, at the very least. You can't find anything to do with the art side of the studio. Did you send anybody in with any artistic ability?'

'Of course we didn't,' said Jim. 'We would not bother you with this.'

'It's an art studio, Jim. You know, that's what I do,' said Sabine. 'You guys are wild. You really are—bloody crack me up. Art studio. Oh, maybe we could get somebody from the art department to go in and suss it out, in case there's anything else in there.'

'Trust me,' said Emmett. 'If he had a thought of that, you'd have been first called.'

'Damn right,' laughed Jim, until he suddenly realised that Emmett hadn't meant that as any sort of compliment or fun comment.

'Macleod says we should be careful going after him,' said Sabine, taking a very serious tone. 'He says MacPhail is nasty.'

'Don't go after him. Keep it very low key and back.'

'I'll advise Clarissa,' said Sabine, 'but you know how she is.'

'We don't need interference. It takes time with somebody like MacPhail, to get on top of him, to find out things.'

'OK, send me what you've got on him,' said Sabine.

'Anything for you; you know that.'

Sabine jumped off the edge of his desk and walked out to the door, knowing that Jim was watching her the whole way. When she got into the corridor, Emmett shuffled up beside her.

'You okay with that?' he said.

'Yes,' said Sabine, 'you don't need to defend me. I thank you for it, but you don't need to do it. I was playing him. Trust me, I'm fortunate enough that I have a figure that makes some men do things they wouldn't want to do normally. He gives me information on the quiet, and all because I flash my eyes at him.'

'You shouldn't have to do that, though,' said Emmett.

'You live in a very different world, I think,' said Sabine.

'It wouldn't work on me.'

'No?' said Sabine. 'You never had a girl that could play you?'

'I had one once, but she didn't play me. Well, she played me at board games.'

'Fair enough,' said Sabine. She strode back to the office and Emmett joined her. His desk was still not set up properly, and there were two cardboard boxes sitting on it.

'We'll visit Stewart,' said Ferguson, 'but when we do it, you'll keep a low profile. You're our trump card in some ways. Nobody knows you. In the meantime, why don't you get set up here, and I'll take you out for something to eat. We're going to be working together, Emmett. We could do with knowing each other better.'

'I'm sorry if I overstepped. I just thought he was out of line.'

'He was. And you were decent enough to defend me. But when people are out of line, and they think they're in charge, is often where you get the most out of them. I'm not like Clarissa, I'm not in their face. I'm very subtle and I will work people. You need to follow that lead.'

'Understood,' said Emmett.

'And I need to follow whatever leads you give me,' said Sabine, 'so I need to know you.'

She sat down in her chair. 'Unpack your stuff and we'll go out afterwards.' Sabine lay back in the seat and watched him as various knickknacks were put out on the table. An array of tiny figures were produced. Sabine stared at them. Some of them looked like weird knight spacemen. There was a creature that she couldn't even describe. Something had wings. One looked like a vampire. None of them were more than an inch or two high, incredibly well painted. All delicately done.

'What are those?' she asked.

'When I need to think, I paint. I do my models. I'm part of the gaming group.' Emmett produced a small box and opened it to show the paints inside.

'You wanted to know me. This is me. It's what I do. I paint. I guess somebody like Jim would call me a geek, a nerd, something like that. He'd probably wonder why a forty-year-old man was sitting doing that. Especially when I'm single, why I wouldn't be out at the strip bars or clubs? I take it he's married.'

'Jim? Jim's divorced. It took her ten years to see sense, but she saw it.'

'If you want, you could come along to one of our board game nights. You might enjoy it,' offered Emmett, almost smiling.

'I don't know if I would,' said Sabine. 'I'm more the athletic type. But I'll come. In fact, we'll all go. Clarissa as well.'

'She doesn't like to lose, though, does she?' said Emmett warily. 'She's still seething over this breakfast thing with Macleod. I could pick that much up.'

'You're right there. She doesn't like to lose.'

Sabine sat back, pondering on Emmett. He picked a lot up. He said very little, and he picked a lot up. Macleod didn't bring people into places for no reason. She wondered what he was doing here. Maybe Emmett was going to give the team something that wasn't there already. She smiled. He was a nice guy. You didn't get nice guys that often.

Chapter 09

We should have gone to Glasgow, Pats. Do you know that?'

'Why?' asked Patterson, sitting in the passenger seat of the little green car as it raced its way towards Aberdeen.

'Well, what have we done today? We spent the day going to addresses that basically were empty. People don't live there anymore. I mean, what sort of address book did this guy have? Did he ever update it?'

'Do you ever update yours?' asked Patterson.

'I don't have an address book. I have the phone now.'

'Do you ever update the phone? Do you ever go in and change addresses in it?'

'You don't need to, do you? I mean, you just look people up. It's easier these days. Back when I had a proper address book, back when I was in the business, looking around for art, when you had to have people's numbers, I had a properly maintained book. My address book was a work of art itself.'

'I've no doubt it was,' said Patterson, almost absentmindedly.

'What's that meant to mean?'

'Nothing. Nothing at all,' said Patterson, not wishing to look back at Clarissa.

'Sometimes I think you forget that I'm the boss. You say nice things to your boss. You sort of keep them on side, you know? Don't give them any reason not to dislike you.'

'Do you dislike me then?' said Patterson.

'You brought me the greatest trauma of my life.'

'Well, excuse me for dying,' said Patterson.

'Anyway,' said Clarissa, 'we have to turn you into an arts expert, and this isn't helping. If we'd been down in Glasgow, we'd probably go and see dealerships or whatever. Could have taken you in, introduced you.'

'This is important,' said Patterson. 'This is the trawl. You said we need to find his muse. This is how we find the muse. She's not just going to appear. We're going to have to go through everything.'

'Who's this one we're going to in Aberdeen anyway?' said Clarissa.

'See'am Moon. That's the name on it.'

'Is that a man or a woman?'

'I haven't got a clue,' said Patterson.

'Come on, Pats. I'm bringing the expertise here on the arts front. Least you could do is pick up the names.'

Patterson resisted the temptation to push his arm forward as Clarissa whipped round a corner at a speed that Patterson wasn't sure was totally safe. She slowed down somewhat when they reached Aberdeen, having to negotiate the various traffic in the streets until she pulled up in front of a small set of apartments.

As they stepped out, they stood for a moment, watching. The apartments weren't classy by any means, set inside a granite building. But then again, that's the city they were in. Aberdeen wasn't the most beautiful city Clarissa had ever been in, but it had its moments. In fact, it had plenty of moments. But it was a working city.

'What floor did it say?' asked Clarissa.

'Three.'

'Three. It's never the ground floor, is it? I mean, it's never the right-in-front-of-you ground floor. Anyway, it looks like rain,' said Clarissa. 'Let's get inside.'

Patterson followed his boss, dressed in her tartan trews and her lady boots, tartan shawl wrapped around her. She looked tired, Patterson thought. And they were covering a lot of miles. He also thought she was annoyed at being away. This art job differed from the murder squad. With the murder squad, you seem to go to a place, or you might have been working long hours out of Inverness Base. This was less a one centre operation. More multi centres. The art world was small but being spread out across the country.

'Is there a lift?' asked Clarissa as they walked into the entrance hall of the apartments.

'There's one over there, but can you hear that?'

Clarissa cocked an ear towards the staircase on her right-hand side. 'Somebody's not happy. How far up would you say that is?'

Patterson shrugged his shoulders. 'How far up can I hear that from? I don't know,' he said; 'it's up there.'

'I'll take the stairs then.'

They strode towards the stairs, and the row above them increased. They could hear a woman's voice and a man who sounded low and menacing. It was difficult to catch the words, but as they drew closer, it wasn't a pleasant conversation.

Clarissa tried not to huff and puff as she made the third-floor landing, where she could instantly see what the problem was.

A woman was surrounded by three men. She stood with her back to the open door of a flat behind her. However, the three men were not in a cheerful mood. One of them was clearly threatening physical violence. They were dressed, however, in casual suits.

He said, 'You'll be coming with us. You understand that, don't you? No point running.'

The man speaking was tall, maybe six feet, and Clarissa thought he looked reasonably strong. The girl he was talking to—for she was a girl in Clarissa's eyes—was maybe only twenty at most. She had long black hair, but more than that, she had features that looked homely. Girl next door! Clarissa reckoned she knew the face.

'Wow,' said Patterson, as he caught a look at the girl. But not from a physical point of view, in the sense that he liked her, but the uncanny resemblance to the sculptures back in Kylesku.

'That's her, boss,' said Patterson.

'And she looks like she's in trouble,' whispered Clarissa. She walked forward towards the group of men surrounding the woman.

'Are you all right, love?' asked Clarissa, innocently.

'Piss off, Grandma. It's not your business, all right? Just sod off.'

'That's not the way to speak to an older woman.'

Cheers, Pats, thought Clarissa. *Older woman just makes me feel so good.*

'I asked her. I asked the girl, "Was she okay?"' said Clarissa.

'And I told you to piss off,' said one of the men. 'Now take your son here and sod off back to wherever you came from, if you know what's good for you.'

'I want to talk to this young woman,' said Clarissa.

'Look at you,' said the man, 'look at the state of you, granny. What are you, a national exhibit for Scotland? Look at those bloody trousers. You're like a piss-take of our national identity.'

Patterson drew in his breath sharply; this would not go well. Clarissa said nothing; she simply marched on the man. Her shoulders were forward and she was driving from her boots, shawl flapping behind her. The man was caught by surprise but he got both hands out and pushed her backward.

'Do you want me to—?' said the man beside him. But Clarissa had already taken exception to the man's shove and kicked him hard in the knee.

The third man reached across, grabbing the young woman by the throat. And Patterson sprinted forward. The third man reached towards Patterson, but Patterson pushed him back against a wall as the first man bent over, holding his knee, swearing loudly. Clarissa went to make a move towards him, but he turned on her, producing a gun from his pocket.

'I don't have time for this, Grandma. You understand that? You pushed it too far, way too far.'

Patterson swallowed, still holding his man against the wall, as the gun was swinging back and forward in front of Clarissa.

'Everybody's going to go inside,' said the man. 'We're all going to go inside and sit down, because some of us have taken it too far. Some of us don't know when to shut up. Some of us . . .'

Clarissa wasn't someone to listen to fools. The man was blabbering away, trying to exert dominance again after receiving a kick from an elderly woman, or a national relic as he saw it. What he didn't see was Clarissa's hands were underneath her shawl, finding the nightstick tucked up inside. Macleod had said it could be rough, and while Clarissa never armed herself with a gun, she armed herself with other things.

In a quick motion, she pulled the night stick out, letting it extend once clear of her shawl. Without stopping the swing, she brought it to bear on the man's hand, striking him hard, causing the hand to reflex open, and the gun to drop on the floor. As it hit the ground, Clarissa kicked it hard, sending it spiralling of to the stairs and tumbling down.

'You bitch,' said the man. He reached forward and Clarissa swung the nightstick again, but this time he was ready for it, grabbing it and pulling Clarissa towards him.

Patterson received a headbutt from the man he was holding against the wall, causing him to stumble backwards. But as the man looked to follow up on him, Patterson stepped to one side, sweeping his leg, catching him around the ankles and sending the man to the ground.

Clarissa, meanwhile, had been grabbed by the man facing her. He was holding her by the throat. However, her hands had shot up, grabbing him first by the hair, pulling it hard, and then shoving her thumbs up towards his eyes. He pushed her back roughly, yelling in pain, and Clarissa stumbled backwards until her back hit the railing that protected the stairs.

The man looked at her and charged forward. Clarissa waited, and then spun to one side, causing the man to run straight into the metal railing. He yelled, stumbling backwards from it.

Patterson was up on his feet, and now grappling with the man who was holding the girl. He was shorter than the other two, but he was strong. Patterson, however, freed an arm, which allowed the woman to drive an elbow straight into the man's gut. With Patterson pulling on him, she slipped away and ran towards the stairs.

Clarissa saw the man who had attacked her running to intercept the woman, and threw herself at him, catching him about the knees and knocking him sideways. The girl skipped past, the baggy jumper she was wearing swinging wildly. Her black hair streaked out behind her as she took the stairs two at a time while descending.

The man who Patterson had knocked to the floor was now getting up to run to the stairs after the woman. But Clarissa, still on her feet, bent forward slightly. It had been a long time since her younger days. She remembered tackling the boys at school. She'd watched how they'd executed a tackle. How they put their head to one side, rolled their shoulders in towards the knees. And she did exactly the same.

The man running after the girl was expecting a stand-up fight, but instead he got Clarissa throwing herself at knee height. The tackle was far from pretty, and his knee caught her in the side of the head. But what it did for him was knock him over the top of her, off his feet, and sent him sprawling.

The first man was over towards the window of the flats, looking down.

'She's getting out onto the street. Move it, you two, move it.'

He turned to run for the stairs, and this time got hit in the side by Patterson, who sent him once again into the railings. But the third man caught Patterson unawares, catching him right under his chin with a flashing uppercut. Patterson spun backwards.

Clarissa was on the floor, and as the men began to run down the stairs, the first one, who had pointed the gun at her, turned for a moment to look at her. He raised his foot, Clarissa prone on the floor, and then drove his leg down hard at her face. Clarissa, despite her age, had an awareness to her, and she saw the move coming from a mile away. Because of this, she could spin slightly to one side and his foot landed right beside her head.

But she wasn't finished. As the foot landed, she flung an arm around his leg, refusing to let him lift it back up. She rolled into his leg and bit it, her teeth sinking through the fabric of his trouser, deep into his flesh. The man howled in agony. He shook his leg desperately, but she hung on. *Like a rottweiler*, she thought to herself.

She hoped that Patterson would get up soon, because she wouldn't hold the man on her own.

'Hey, bitch!' he shouted. 'Damn grandma!' Patterson didn't get up and the man shook Clarissa until she could no longer hang on. She rolled away from him, banking on the fact he needed to get out after the girl. Otherwise, he could follow up, put a kick into her while she was prone on the ground. As she rolled, she caught a look at his face. He was coming. He was coming for her.

'An old woman,' said a voice beside her. Patterson was back on his feet. He looked groggy.

'Next time, grandma. Next time I'll have you.'

'Don't call me grandma,' said Clarissa. 'Next time I take half that leg off.' It was bravado. She was exhausted and sore, but bravado was all she had left.

The man looked at Patterson and raced for the stairs.

'Get after them, Pats; get after them, get a plate, get something,' shouted Clarissa, wheezing.

'Are you?'

'Don't worry about me. Go!' she shouted.

Patterson took off down the stairs and Clarissa rolled onto her knees. She made her way across to the metal stanchion that protected the stairs. Hauling herself up onto her feet, she made her way to the window to look down at the street below. She saw Patterson clearly moving from side to side as he ran. He'd need to get checked out; he could be concussed. Yet he was in full flow.

A car suddenly drove the other way. A man in a suit—the one who had pointed the gun at her—got into the car, and they roared away. She couldn't see the girl anywhere.

Clarissa breathed in deeply. It had all happened so quickly, so fast. She hobbled along. more from a lack of breath than anything else. Slowly, she made her way down the stairs.

She saw the gun, a flight down, took out a tissue and wrapped it up, pocketing it. As she made the second floor, a door opened across from her. A young woman approached.

Are you all right?' said the woman. 'I heard the fracas. I didn't want to come out. We need to get you to a hospital. Have you got a son or a daughter I can call? Have you got someone to look after you? Attacking someone of your age. It's . . .'

'DI Clarissa Urquhart,' said Clarissa determinedly. 'I'm a police officer. And I'm fine; just a scuffle.'

The woman beside her looked at her for a moment and Clarissa thought the woman had decided she was delirious or off her mind. She reached inside the shawl and pulled out a warrant card. 'I am DI Clarissa Urquhart. Thank you for your help but I'm fine. I may be older than you, but I know how to handle myself.'

Patterson arrived on the landing. 'I'm sorry, boss; couldn't get them. She's gone too. Run off. She'll know the area. I don't think they were going after her though; they were just getting away. They reckon this place is going to be crawling with uniform soon. That's where they're headed. Glasgow accents, no? Did you clock that?'

'I clocked it all right,' said Clarissa. She looked over at him. 'Are you all right? You seem to be—'

'Caught me with a hell of an uppercut.'

'Take DC Patterson inside,' she said to the woman. 'Give him a seat for a moment; get him some water. Pats, just let yourself stop for a moment. I'll call it in, get some uniform to help us and then we'll go up and find out just who this See'am Moon was.'

'We know who she was,' said Patterson. 'There's no mistake in it. She's the Muse.'

'Is that some sort of police code?' said the woman beside them. *She didn't even understand the word Muse*, thought Clarissa. *What's the world coming to? I mean, she's not that young. She must be in her twenties.* Patterson allowed the woman to give him a hand and take him inside while Clarissa phoned Aberdeen Police Station.

She then leaned against the railings of the stairway. They were close. So close. But somebody was after the sculptor's muse. It seemed more and more likely. Ernesto was in big trouble. Just what sort of trouble? She didn't know.

Chapter 10

S abine Ferguson stood in front of the mirror. She looked sharp in long black trousers, a white blouse, and a short jacket. There was a broad-brimmed hat on top as well. Sabine wasn't one for fashion, happiest when slouching around. Happier still when she was in her training gear, running on a treadmill, working out in the gym. But this called for a bit of class. She needed to look like she was an arts dealer.

When Sabine normally went to look at artworks, she was dressed extremely casually, but every now and again, she had to make herself up. She hated it. She rarely put make-up on during her daily life.

One boyfriend that she'd had told her she didn't need it. He was a special sort, one she was sad to lose when he emigrated. And although they kept in touch with letters, it wasn't enough to keep the relationship going. They'd stayed friends, although they were very distant friends.

His best feature was that he had never told her she'd looked good if she hadn't. He told her the truth. She remembered putting her make-up on that time, and when she arrived, she asked him how she looked. He looked, and he told her—done up, ruined what she was. He wasn't being kind; he was being honest, brutally honest, and it was an honesty she wasn't too sure she wanted at that time, but she'd learnt to value it.

She never wore make-up around him, but it also gave her a confidence that she looked the part with none on. She thanked him for that. Now, however, she had lipstick on, her eyebrows were coloured in and her eyelashes, longer than any she'd ever imagined. She didn't look good. She looked made up. But the type of woman she was going to play would love her look.

'How do I look, Emmett?'

Emmett Grump, by contrast, was wearing a large parka, despite the fact it was the back end of summer. He wasn't wearing make-up either. His trousers looked rather dull and he could have blended in on any street or in any mode of public transport. He was a man that didn't have money. That's what it said. He was also his usual quiet self.

'You look the part,' he said.

'Had a boyfriend once said I didn't need make-up.'

'Most women don't need make-up,' said Emmett. 'I don't know any man that asked for women to wear make-up.' It was very matter of fact the way he spoke.

'Jim likes his women wearing make-up.'

'Jim doesn't like women,' said Emmett. 'He likes dolls.'

Sabine stared at Emmett. A rather strange comment. 'Dolls?' she said.

'He turns you into dolls. Things to play with. I said he doesn't like women.'

Sabine was taking her time to get to know Emmett. The man was quiet, pleasant enough, and never rude. Yet he kept himself very much to himself. He helped with the investigation, forthcoming with any ideas, absolutely. He certainly wasn't shirking his job. But he wasn't a brilliant conversationalist. So very quiet.

'So your plan is, if we review it,' said Sabine, 'that I go in and I can catch their eye, talk to them about the pieces, elicit what I can about the studio. See if I can find some works by Ernesto. And you're going to do what?'

'Look for an opportunity,' said Emmett, 'to find out more.'

'Do you want to expand on that?' asked Sabine. 'In case I need to play off you.'

'You don't need to play off me,' said Emmett. 'You just need to engage them, find out what you can. Learn as much as you can about what they'll say about Ernesto Hunter and any pieces they have from him. I'll try to get behind the organisation somehow.'

'You want to flesh that out more for me,' said Sabine, 'because I need to set the path.'

'No. They don't know me. You're in the Glasgow office,' said Emmett. 'If they recognise you, you deal with antiques. What does it matter? You could just be in looking for antiques. You're plausible. I'm a nobody. If I get caught poking into things, I'm a nobody. I blend into the background, Sabine. People don't look at me and think, "Oh, I want to talk to him, he's interesting." I'm a geek.'

Sabine thought about the little figures now sitting on Emmett's desk. Earlier on today, he'd been painting some of them. She knew that two other officers in the building had grunted about them, asking what he was doing with kids' stuff. But the quality of the paintwork, that wasn't by a kid. Sure, it wasn't what Sabine was into, but Emmett took great care and attention with it.

'Okay. I'll run with it, but we need to come back with

something. Clarissa doesn't mess about. She wants results.'

'Oh, I can see that about her. She's very forward. Very . . . dynamic.'

Sabine laughed. Surely, he was being polite. 'She's that all right. Shall we go?'

'I'll get the bus down. Shall we say you enter round about two? I'll come in about five past. Make sure you capture their attention.'

'Do we know who works there though?' asked Sabine. 'We know there's this Janice Stewart running the place—MacPhail's new girlfriend—but who else is in it? What do the reports say?'

'There's a young lad works with them, and another woman. If we're in luck, it'll be the young lad that's in, and the other woman won't be about.'

'Why's that?' asked Sabine.

'Young lad, early twenties, hormones through the roof, probably. You'll grab his eye. He won't be looking at me and if you're spending money, hopefully, you'll grab Janice's eye, too.'

'And if the other woman's there?'

'I'll just have to be quick,' said Emmett. 'Don't worry, I can roll with it. See what comes.'

Sabine nodded and took her car from the rear of the Glasgow station, parking it a little distance away from the shop. She watched her time, waiting until the clock got round to about two before walking the short distance to the shop. The shop window was a large glass front and you could see deep into the office. But the showroom swung round a corner, deeper inside.

As Sabine entered, a bell rang somewhere, clearly showing

someone entered the shop, and a young man appeared from around the corner.

'Hello, madam,' he said. 'Can I help you?'

'Well, I'm just looking for some pieces, actually. Something to go in my new living room. And is that by Ernesto Hunter?' asked Sabine, pointing across the shop.

The man looked across, and he slowly made his way over, catching the label underneath it. It was only then that he turned and nodded. 'Yes, it is,' he said.

He's an amateur, she thought. *He doesn't know.*

'I have to say, that's quite something, wouldn't you say? Look at the lines in that work. Which would you say would be the best feature?'

Despite his standing up fully, Sabine was a couple of inches taller than the man. She could see his eyes scanning her. Emmett's plan was a good one, so far. But then she saw a woman appear at the corner. She would have been in her very early thirties, with long blonde hair. She had a skirt that ran to just above the knee. It was about as much as you could get away with in a shop like this. Her blouse was tight and showed off her figure. But it wasn't overly provocative. It spoke of class, by all means, with sexual undertones. But it was class.

'Who've we got here, Jeremy?' said the woman. 'Hello, madam. Delighted to have you here. You're looking at the Ernesto Hunter piece?'

The piece was of a woman lying on a couch and Sabine recognised who the woman was. But alongside it, were many other pieces as well.

'The nursery was a favourite of mine. Have you many pieces of his?' Sabine had a quick glance around. 'This is one, but I don't see any others.'

'Quite hard to get hold of. I'm sure we could get you one. I also have a direct line in to him if you want to get a commission.'

'A commission? That would cost a bit, wouldn't it? I'm not sure I can afford that at the moment, although I could afford this piece.'

Sabine looked down at the price tag. She couldn't afford this piece on her current salary. But never let something like that stop a good lie.

'What's this over here?' said Sabine, and she marched deeper into the studio so she could see round the corner. There was a desk with a small computer on top, and beyond that, an office of some sort, led into by a wooden door in the wall. A window showed that there were filing cabinets, and more computers inside. However, Sabine couldn't see anyone else in the shop.

Just then, she heard the bell ring again. Janice Stewart walked to the corner, peered around, and asked in a rather abrupt tone if she could help someone there. Sabine heard Emmett's voice.

'Just looking,' he said.

'Please don't touch,' she said. 'If you need to see anything, do call me.' Janice turned her attention back to Sabine.

'This piece here, that's quite something, isn't it? It's small.'

'It's quite pricey though, isn't it?' said Sabine. 'Is it an original?'

'Chambers,' she said. 'Yes, always holds its value, does a Chambers.'

Sabine looked at it. It was good. Very good. Very much in Chambers style. 'Can I hold it?'

'We don't let just anyone touch the items. But, of course, you may hold it and examine it. A woman of your class and obvious knowledge.'

Sabine picked up the small item, turning it over. It was good. Extremely good. But Sabine wasn't happy. Something didn't feel right. A Chambers? She wished she had Clarissa with her. Between the two of them, they could work out what was wrong with it. Something just didn't sit right.

She caught a glance at Emmett. His eyes flicked out towards the front door. Sabine looked over and saw a large Trojan horse sculpture. It was massive enough that you could have hidden four or five people inside it.

'Look at that,' said Sabine, and marched over with the young boy and Janice in her wake.

She stood there, letting Janice brief her about what it was. Unfortunately, it was already bought and would ship out soon.

'It's quite something though, isn't it?'

The doorbell went again. Janice turned and along with Sabine saw Emmett looking like he was about to leave. Janice flicked her head back quickly. Sabine could see that she was focused on Sabine and the potential that she might purchase something. The young lad was staring, mouth drooped at Sabine.

The door closed, but Emmett was still inside. The man raced along behind her and Sabine did her best not to follow him with her eyes, instead pointing at the Trojan horse, discussing it with the owner in front of her. Emmett disappeared round the corner of the shop, then was out of sight, and Sabine walked forward to look at another item towards the front of the shop.

For ten minutes, she stood talking about different pieces. Most of them seemed very genuine, but several of them she was struggling with the authenticity. It was her questioning mind. If she'd been randomly walking into a Sotheby's or a well-known auction house, she wouldn't question it. Here, in her mind, she was trying to validate everything. If there were questions, even if there were any nagging doubts, she wouldn't allow herself to see that piece as definitely genuine.

There were lots of pieces she wasn't sure about. The Ernesto Hunter piece, however, was different. Definitely genuine. She so wished she had Clarissa with her. As she stood talking to Janice, she saw Emmett appear at the back of the showroom. He snuck up behind and Sabine did her best to keep Janice and the young lad focused on her. Emmett pulled the door open quickly, jumping back outside and then poking his head back in.

Janice turned, looking at him. 'Back again,' she said. 'Was there something?'

'I'm sorry, I dropped something. I don't know if I dropped it here.'

'What was it?'

'Just a glove. Is there a glove on the floor? I can't see one. I was only here, around the front of the shop. It's just, it's, well, I'm not sure I can afford another one.'

'You've dropped nothing here, love,' said Janice. 'Maybe it was before you came in. We've been walking around here for the last ten to fifteen minutes and there's nothing here. I'm sorry.'

'Well, thank you,' said Emmett. 'That's very kind.' He disappeared out of the shop.

Sabine stayed for another twenty minutes getting details of various items. She let it be known that she'd never seen the studio before, and Janice said it had not been open for long. She'd had trouble gaining pieces for such a size of showroom, but now she'd successfully managed it. Sabine nodded and told her she'd be back as a few of the items had quite struck her. She took one more look at the Trojan horse.

'I wouldn't mind that,' she said.

'Of course not. Who wouldn't? That's why it's gone,' said Janice. 'But please, come back. Here's my card.' She passed over a card with the name of the studio on it, and Sabine pocketed it.

'I'll call ahead to let you know I'm coming,' said Sabine.

'Please do. We could be better prepared. I may have some champagne. We do occasionally have evenings where an artist comes in. We can show off their work. You'd be more than welcome.'

'That would be delightful,' said Sabine. She made her way back to her car and found a text message from Emmett, saying he'd meet her back at the station. When she got there, approximately fifteen minutes later, Emmett was already back at his desk. He sat with a small miniature in his hands. A gargoyle and he was examining the back of it. It was painted entirely in white.

'It's a base layer. I still need to do the detail on it.' He put it down.

'How did it go?' she said.

'You, first.'

'Well, the pieces are good, but I'm not sure about a lot of them. I would like to have Clarissa in with me. I can't pin anything down definitely, but some of them, it's just, it's a hunch; it's a feeling.'

'Well,' said Emmett, 'I got into their computer files. I photographed their entire catalogue before I came out. MacPhail's bought several pieces from them. But he has bought nothing that was worked by Ernesto Hunter. It's all other artists. You can read them. I think he bought that massive horse thing as well.'

'Trojan horse. It's from—'

'Mythology. Greek mythology. You don't have to tell me about mythology. I'm a board gamer. I live on mythology,' said Emmett.

'Something in common,' said Sabine. Mythology was important to her because so many of the old artworks were based on it. She smiled at him. 'Is there anything untoward with the records, though?'

'Not that I can see. Everything looks to be paid for. I can see why they checked for money laundering with the amount of money MacPhail was putting through the place, but they said that wasn't the case. Maybe he just likes his artwork.'

'I don't think so,' said Sabine. 'Something's up. We need to talk to Clarissa. I might need her to come and check some of these items for me.'

Chapter 11

Clarissa had left Patterson in the back of an ambulance, getting checked out. There was a bruise on his chin developing. By all standards, it seemed to have been a cracking punch he'd received. However, he'd been in worse situations, which she remembered only too well.

Clarissa couldn't rest, though, and had gone up to see the flat of See'am Moon. Her neighbours were nosing at events, especially with the police presence that arrived. Clarissa decided she should interview them. The flat was guarded so that no one could enter, and Clarissa needed to think about bringing in a forensic unit.

The neighbours directly beside See'am Moon were an elderly couple. The man who had fought with Clarissa would have probably thought them ancient if he thought Clarissa was a grandma. The old woman had white hair and a lazy eye on one side, but she was positively lovely, Clarissa thought. Her husband guarded her, for the man was bold, quite squat, and only gave way to his wife to speak. Though Clarissa could see he was observing her. Maybe she was frail, but for whatever reason, he cast a careful eye over Clarissa.

'See'am's been here for over a year. Lovely girl. She's quite beautiful, isn't she? She would disappear, at times, for a week, maybe. Quite far away. She said she had a friend who lived the other side of the country. She never said where she went, but we know she would get the bus across to Inverness. After that, I'm not sure.'

'Did she have a lot of money?' asked Clarissa.

'I'm not sure what she did for work. She paid rent, for we all rent these flats, and she obviously had enough. Mrs Anderson, she rents them. Lives in the downstairs flat.'

Clarissa had seen an agitated middle-aged woman talking at length with the uniformed sergeant who had turned up.

'Did she ever have visitors in?'

'No, kept herself to herself. But I did see something. I fell once,' said the old woman, 'and See'am brought me in. Derek here was out and See'am brought me into her apartment. I was sitting down on her sofa and there was like a figurine on top of her telly. Proper old telly. She didn't have the new ones. One of the old ones, so you could place something on top.'

'What was special about the figurine?' asked Clarissa.

'It was her,' said the old woman. 'It was quite beautiful. I don't know what it was made from, some sort of stone. Didn't get to pick it up, so I don't know if it was heavy, if it was porcelain or that. I'm not that way inclined. Don't know about that stuff, but I know what I was looking at, and it was beautiful. She was proud of it, I think, but also a little embarrassed.'

'Why embarrassed,' asked Clarissa, 'if it was beautiful?'

'She was nude. I'm an old woman. Nudity. I've seen it all,' she said. She laughed, turning to Derek. 'We've seen each other when we were splendid, and we've seen each other now, when the bag is a bit worn.' She laughed. 'See'am was beautiful; that figurine, too. She obviously had posed for it with someone. I asked her who, and she said a friend. But those eyes said they were more than friends. I don't mean, necessarily they were partners or lovers or anything. It was that other look, the look of deep friendship, special friendship. Do you know?'

'The way I look at her,' said Derek. 'Because that's what you need, isn't it? Because you can't look at the exterior. We all get our lumps and bumps. We all get old. If all you're doing is looking at the exterior, you're going to be pretty disappointed after several years. There must be something good inside. Otherwise, all you've got is what wasn't there before.'

'He's got such a way with words, hasn't he?' said the woman. She laughed. 'He's right, though. When you're young, you see all the outside, don't you? If you're really lucky, you capture the inside too.'

Clarissa nodded. She loved Frank. She loved his face, especially. But he wasn't an Adonis. And neither was she a goddess. Well, maybe a goddess of war if you believed Macleod.

'Did she have anybody visit?'

'No. No one. But she wasn't hiding from anyone. She would talk to us, her neighbours. Would say hello when we came past. She came in here a few times to check up if we were okay. There was a time when Derek had to go into hospital for a couple of days. Nothing serious. Just had to be in hospital. And she asked him before he went if he wanted her to drop in and just check I was fine. And she did it. She was a good neighbour. Nice person. Very nice person.'

'See'am Moon. Have you ever heard the name See'am before?'

'No. I'll tell you something, though. Twice I called to her, and I thought she was deaf. I said, "See'am, See'am," and she didn't respond. She never seemed to have trouble hearing anything else.'

Clarissa nodded and thanked the couple. *Maybe it wasn't the real name*, she thought. After checking if Patterson was all right, and being told the paramedics would require a little more time with him, Clarissa entered the flat.

There was a small sofa, an old one, in front of a television, and Clarissa saw the sculpture. It was an Ernesto Hunter one for sure, and it was beautiful. It was deeply intimate, too. Not just the figure, but the face.

Clarissa wandered on round and put on a pair of gloves as she searched through drawers. Most of the flat was very basic, quite nondescript. A few cups, some plates. A fridge that had little in it. Clothing-wise, there was next to nothing. Certainly, you would expect there to be more. Did she have a stash bag somewhere else?

It looked like a person who might have to clear out soon. Either that or someone who had so very little. And yet, some of what she had was of a price that you would expect her to have more obvious wealth. Some of the little extras of life. Like some magazines, comics, DVDs. The golf clubs that Frank had.

The flat just looked like it wasn't lived in that often. It looked like a place you were expecting to leave. The theme continued until Clarissa got into the bedroom.

There was a small set of drawers beside the bed, and in the bottom drawer were several photograph albums. Clarissa pulled them out and began looking through. There were photographs of what she thought were camps. Young people together. Smiles everywhere. She couldn't find See'am in many of them. There was a priest that seemed to appear in quite a few. Even the odd nun. And some of the same children appeared many times.

But she couldn't see any of See'am. She opened the top drawer and there was a Bible, and a cross. There were also some religious books, religious poetry. She looked through them and in the Bible, Clarissa found an inscription, from Father Kershaw, made out to Cara Mackey.

Clarissa took a photograph before placing the items carefully back where she had found them. She returned to the photographs and at the back of one album, in a separate slip, she found ten individual photographs. Seven of them were pictures of Hunter's work.

Clarissa recognised the style, and all of them were of See'am. The other three pictures, however, showed Hunter in his studio. He was smiling in them, but only one included See'am. She was sitting on the chaise longue in the studio, wrapped up in a long sheet, sitting beside him. His arm wasn't around her. Instead, they were leaning up against each other, shoulders touching.

There was nothing erotic about the photograph, nothing sexual. It was like two friends, just doing what they loved. Clarissa took photographs with her mobile phone before placing them back again. *Cara Mackey*, she thought. *Something to go on. And Father Kershaw.*

Clarissa made her way down the stairs and back out to the ambulance. Patterson was sitting on the edge of the bed in the ambulance, with a paramedic sitting close by.

'How's the boxer, then?' asked Clarissa.

'He's taken quite a blow, but I can't see any concussion. We've done our checks. I think he'll be fine, but maybe you should be driving.'

'I must be near death,' said Patterson, 'if they're suggesting you drive.'

There was the quip. He was all right then, was Pats. Able to throw in a dig at her.

'Well, if you're fit and ready, get your backside out of this ambulance and come and start earning your money,' said Clarissa.

Patterson gave her a grin before walking past. He stopped at the edge of the ambulance, turned and thanked the paramedic inside. When he'd gone, Clarissa turned back to the paramedic.

'Thank you; he took quite a blow to the chin.'

'He's going to have a cracking bruise across the bone there. It might not come out too deep because it was on the bone. You know how these things go.'

'I do,' she said.

As she turned away, the paramedic looked at her. 'And are you okay?'

'Well, I didn't get punched like he did.'

'No, but he said that you were involved in the fracas. He said you were on the ground biting a man's leg.'

'I was.'

'We should check you out, especially if you got pushed about.'

'No need,' said Clarissa. 'I'm a rottweiler. I don't play fair. And when I play dirty, I bite hard.'

The paramedic looked at her, and Clarissa realised she hadn't a clue what she was talking about. Outside, Patterson was standing in the street.

'What have we got?' he asked. 'I take it you've been everywhere and done everything while I was sitting in there?'

'She's gone, Pats,' said Clarissa. 'She may not be See'am Moon, either but a Cara Mackey. Her flat is rather devoid of character. Very basic. Very few clothes as well. I think she was someone who was ready to run. I don't know why. That's the problem. I don't know why she's here.

'She has a Bible, which has an inscription from a Father Kershaw. So that's where we go first. Find out where he is. Also check the name Cara Mackey. We've got photographs of happy times, but they're all in camps. They're all away from a home life. There's no family life photographed. There are also some special photographs of Hunter's work. And there's one photograph of Hunter and her. A couple more of Hunter himself.'

'What sort of photograph?'

'Friends. This relationship between them is more than friendship, though. She's . . . I don't know what she is. She's obviously quite comfortable with him, quite comfortable doing the nude work. That would suggest a deep level of friendship, especially if she's not intimate with him. You saw that photograph. There's no way they're intimate. She also might be quite devout. I wonder if she was in church camps because there are priests and nuns in the pictures.'

'If you're telling me we're looking for a religious girl who poses for a sculptor, that would suggest she will not be telling many people about it.'

'Because?' asked Clarissa.

'If you're in a church environment, certainly any I've known, you don't discuss nude modelling. Especially anything where you have to take your clothes off as much as she did. Innocent as it may be, most people wouldn't find that innocent.'

'Philistines,' said Clarissa.

'Maybe,' said Patterson.

'There's no maybe about it. We're talking about high art,

quality,' said Clarissa.

'Either way, I don't think she's going to have told many people about it. If she's using a different name, she will not tell many people she's Cara Mackey, if indeed that's her.'

'We pull the team together,' said Clarissa, 'see what they've got down that end, and then we get after Kershaw.'

'Well, let's get back to the hotel and contact Sabine, but I need to get some ice on this chin as well.'

Clarissa reached over, grabbed Patterson's chin and pulled it towards her to have a look.

'Ow! Good job you were never a doctor.'

'Ah, you've had worse,' she said. 'Maybe next time, you'll avoid the punch.'

'I was two on one at the time, and I stopped you getting a battering.'

'You did, Pats. But if you didn't do that for your boss, I wouldn't have you on my team, anyway. Now quit whining and let's get to work.'

Patterson shook his head.

That's becoming a trait, thought Clarissa, and one that she wasn't too happy about. She needed to have respect from him, not a constant head shake. Then she realised how Macleod must feel whenever she was in the office with him.

Chapter 12

Y ou got that working, Pats?'

There it was, that little shake of the head again, but Patterson had the laptop up and running. They were in Clarissa's room and she made sure that Patterson had aimed the laptop well away from the clothes strewn out on the bed. She had a lot with her and the second pair of tartan trews were being adjusted. In the fight, some part of her trouser had caught, and she was going to have to sew it up.

'Sabine and Emmett are on,' said Patterson; 'however, we're still waiting for the boss.'

'He'll be on time,' said Clarissa. 'He's always on time with these things. But he'll be sitting there flummoxed despite the fact we've told him frequently to just get somebody else to do it. Seoras will always try to do it himself first. And he always screws it up. He's just not a technology person. And he hasn't got Ross anymore. The secretary won't do it until he asks. That's the problem. Do you know that? And often he won't ask her if he's given her a load of work to do.'

'Well, he's not here yet.'

Clarissa sat down in front of the laptop, allowing Patterson to sit on a seat beside her. She stared at the screen and saw

Sabine.

'Hi, where's Emmett?' asked Clarissa.

'He's right beside me here,' Sabine adjusted the screen, and Emmett was seen behind the desk holding up a small figurine.

'What the heck's that?' asked Clarissa.

'It's a gorgon,' said Emmett.

'A gorgon? What do you mean "it's a gorgon"? Where did you get that? Was it at the studio?'

'No,' said Emmett, 'it's mine. I've just done the base layer, just filling in a bit of the dark.'

'You made it?'

'No, I bought it.' He held it up to the screen, and Clarissa saw the small miniature model. It was indeed covered in white, with a couple of dark patches painted on. 'It'll be a while till I get it finished, but I like to keep it going.'

'What's it doing with you now? We're working.'

'We were waiting for you to come on. It helps me think,' said Emmett flatly.

'It helps you think?'

'Yes, it helps him think,' said Sabine. 'I've seen it at work. You'd probably sit with a coffee. He doesn't. He sits and paints. These little figures; he's very good at them,' said Sabine.

'He's good at what?' said a voice suddenly.

'Seoras, nice of you to join us. Take it the secretary had to log you in again,' said Clarissa.

'I'm here, but he's good at what?' said Macleod.

'I do these figures,' said Emmett. He held it up to the screen. 'You see? This is a gorgon.'

'What's a gorgon?' asked Macleod.

'Seoras, a gorgon is a mythological creature. That's why it's got snakes coming out of its head. You know? Do you not

101

remember the tale?' said Clarissa.

'I deal with enough snakes in life without having to think about imaginary ones,' said Macleod. 'Anyway, are you going to get started?'

'We were waiting for you,' said Clarissa. 'Put it down, Emmett. Stop thinking and start discussing. Right, so where are we?' asked Clarissa. 'I've come to, A dead end in some ways. We checked the address book, had a lot of dead ends, but then we traced a See'am Moon. When we got there, she was surrounded by three heavies, probably from Glasgow. Scuffle ensued and, long story short, See'am escaped from them, and us, and is out there somewhere. The heavies got away, although one's got a severe bite on his leg.'

'A bite? What do you mean "a bite"? Patterson?' asked Macleod.

'Clarissa bit him.'

'How is that apprehending a suspect?' asked Macleod.

'He tried to put his boot on my head when I was on the floor, Seoras. You do that to me, you get bit!'

'Is everybody all right?' asked Macleod.

'Pats has got a cracker on his chin. Massive bruise. Took a blinding uppercut.'

'I'm fine,' said Patterson. 'There's no concussion. Yeah, it's smarting, but other than that, it's fine.'

'Told yous to be careful,' muttered Macleod.

'He had a gun, this guy,' said Clarissa. 'I had my nightstick with me. Took it out of his hands. He went too far, though.'

'What do you mean, "He went too far"? He pulled the gun on you, did he?'

'He called me a grandma, Seoras,' said Clarissa. 'That's why I bit him. Deserved it.'

102

Behind Clarissa, Patterson was shaking his head again.

'Would you stop that?' said Clarissa. 'I'm on the screen with the others. Would you kindly stop shaking your head at me? All right? I'm the boss. I make decisions. I take action. You don't like it? Get out. Otherwise, just sit here. Seoras doesn't need to see you shaking your head.'

'So, did you come up with anything from your visit?' asked Macleod.

'Well, she's got another identity, we think. A Cara Mackey. She looks like she could be religious. Had a Bible and a Father Kershaw signed it. Was made it out to her. The only photographs in the house were of what looked like religious camps. They had priests and nuns at them. You'd probably know more about them,' Clarissa said to Macleod.

'I come from the Isle of Lewis, Clarissa,' said Macleod. 'It's Protestant, you know, Protestant.'

'But you speak that Gaelic, don't you?'

'Ga-lic, not Gal-lic. Scots Gaelic. Yes? Not Irish Gaelic. It's spoken by everybody out in the Outer Hebrides who came from there. The Isle of Lewis is predominantly—in fact, just about all—Protestant. When you shift south, it becomes Catholic. Barra is Catholic.'

'Right,' said Clarissa. 'Never understood you religious types.'

'So, she's come out of a Catholic background of some sort,' said Macleod. 'But there's nothing of family life.'

'Nothing at all. I did do a sweep of the local churches before we convened for this. I had time to give them a quick ring. Apparently, the local St. Joseph's said they saw her there. They identified her by her looks. The priest said there was a girl with a face you would lose yourself in, black hair. Described her figure, too. She came dressed up in straightforward clothing, a jeans, t-shirt, nothing stylish in particular. Never took part or joined in anything except the services.'

'Didn't want to be known then,' said Macleod.

'That's the way I'm reading it,' said Clarissa. 'Her neighbours said she was good to them, but they didn't really get to know her. But she's definitely the muse—statue of her in her own flat. But I don't think she's intimate with Ernesto. They are good friends, though. We had one photograph of the two of them together. They looked like friends, not lovers.'

'What about you, Ferguson?'

'Before you do that,' said Emmett suddenly, 'did you notice?'

'Did I notice what?' asked Clarissa.

'Her name? See'am Moon. Yes?'

'What about it?' asked Clarissa.

'Oh, it's a code, isn't it? It's a code they've chosen. She's Cara Mackey. Cara Mackey. C.M. Capital C. Capital M. Put them together. See-Am.'

'Right, but what's the moon mean then?' asked Clarissa.

'Moon is a synonym for muse. You moon about something if you muse about it.'

'What?' blurted Clarissa.

'He's right,' said Macleod. 'He's right. Brilliant, Emmett. Well done.'

Clarissa glanced around the screen, looking first at Macleod, then looking at Sabine. Sabine's face looked puzzled, too.

'Well done, Emmett,' said Patterson from behind Clarissa.

'Well, if we've all stopped waving the pom-poms and boosting our newest member, we'll get on with the next bit. Sabine, Seoras was asking how you got on,' said Clarissa.

'Got some interesting details from the studio. We managed to distract them.'

'How did you get the details?' Macleod asked.

'They were all on their computer,' said Emmett.

'You broke into their computer?' asked Macleod.

'No, the details were all on their screen. Which was very sloppy. The computer in the back office didn't have a lock on it. During the day, they must work on it but they didn't have a timer lock. So I could just go in and scroll through and leave it back where it was whilst Sabine kept them interested.'

'Right,' said Macleod.

'The thing is,' said Sabine, 'MacPhail has bought a lot of works from Janice. She's also his current girlfriend. So, I'm not sure why he's doing this. It's not money laundering. They've checked him for it. When they knew he was involved with her, it was the first thing they did. We need to know where the artwork's going.'

'But it's all legitimate?' asked Macleod.

'I'm not convinced,' said Sabine. 'To be honest, I could have done with Clarissa with me. Emmett doesn't have the background to know this, but I was looking at the pieces. I looked at them in detail and, well, in Ernesto Hunter's stuff, it's him. They only had one piece, and it was his, clearly. It's not a copy. Some of the other bits, from Chambers to some of the rest, I'm not convinced.

'It's good. If it was in somewhere like Sotheby's or another classy auction house, I wouldn't even question it,' said Sabine, 'but it's not, and I have a feeling about it. I don't think it's genuine. Something inside of me is saying this is not genuine and I can't place why.'

'It's not just the locale where it is?' asked Clarissa.

'No, and I can't put my finger on it.'

'Surely you can,' said Macleod. 'I mean, Clarissa talks about the curve, about the style, the way it's made, the way it's—'

'Seoras, enough. She said she can't say why. This happens. Artwork's not like accountancy. There's a feel to it. Sabine says she doesn't think it's right. She may be correct. Maybe I need to come and see it, too.'

'Well, maybe you do,' said Macleod. 'But what's the plan?'

'Need to find out where the artwork's going,' said Sabine. 'According to the guys at the station, he's never been a big artwork collector. So why has he been buying this artwork? Just because she's his bit of stuff, or is he doing something with it? I would say he would just buy it because of who she is, except this feeling that the pieces are not right, you know? We need to find out where it's going.'

'Will you get on to that then?' said Clarissa.

'One more thing,' said Sabine, 'which interested me. MacPhail has bought this massive Trojan horse.'

'Is that code?' asked Macleod. 'Are you actually talking about—'

'I'm talking about a real Trojan horse. It's a sculpture, it's massive, it's even got a hatch in it. Could be a tight fit, but the hatch is there so that you could probably put three or four people inside it. I'm not sure how big the inside is, or if there is an inside. I didn't get to look at it in detail, but there's definitely a hatch carved into it.'

'And why is this important?'

'It's not; it just struck me,' said Sabine. 'If you were making a Trojan horse, why would you have a hatch? Why have something that big? I mean, it's—'

'What she's saying is, rather elegantly,' said Clarissa, 'and just so you Philistines can understand this, the story isn't there. Troy, if you think about it, when you're going to represent that in art, you wouldn't just do the horse, you would do other things around it. The shock of the Trojan horse is not the fact that it's a Trojan horse, it's just a big wooden horse. It's what happens with it. It's the ladder coming down from underneath. So, you would have it with the hatch lying open, the ladder coming down. You wouldn't have it just as a horse, because then it just looks like a big wooden horse. Tell the story with it. It has to evoke the fear, the shock, the horror, the secrecy of it. It has to say something.'

'Does it not just tell you it's a big hidey horse?' said Patterson.

'Pats, I disagree with you. Do you know that?' said Clarissa. 'I disagree with you. Trust me, I get what Sabine's saying, even if the rest of you don't. I take it you all know the story.'

'Emmett here's good on mythology. He's a board gamer, role-play and stuff,' said Sabine.

'He does what?' asked Macleod.

'Role-play,' said Sabine.

'Is that like what we have to do when they take us on these away days?' said Macleod.

'A bit more exciting than that, sir,' said Emmett.

'It's Seoras. No sir. Tell me more.'

'You pretend to be, maybe a spy, maybe . . . a dungeoneer, maybe you're a goblin, maybe you're a, whatever, a character, and you follow it through. Sometimes I do full dress-up.'

'I think we're getting a little off track here. As much as I'm enjoying Emmett's secret nightlife,' said Clarissa, 'let's pull this back a minute. Sabine, get on to those artworks that are coming out of Janice's studio, okay? Find out where they're going. See if there's an end buyer or anything. Discover if there's anything fishy. You know somebody down there can help with that? You know Dudley Paul, Sabine?'

'Dudley Paul?'

'The Grease.'

'Oh, the Grease.'

'That's a good one to go for,' said Clarissa. 'You know him well enough?'

'Yes. Helps being based down here. Crossed paths on a few minor things.'

'Good. Go for him then. It would be an education for Emmett. I'm going to find this Father Kershaw. See if we can get Cara that way. Now that we know it's Cara. I take it this isn't another pseudonym, Emmett.'

'Doesn't appear to be,' said Emmett. 'Why would you do another one? A bit pointless.'

'And if something's as dear to you as that Bible was, you'd have it made out to yourself. Not to a pseudonym,' said Patterson.

'Grand. That's what we do then. And then we'll touch base again. Oh, by the way, Seoras. Did you get those receipts I scanned in?' asked Clarissa.

'I did,' he said. 'Interesting choice of dining arrangements.'

'Got to keep my team going. Reward them when they do well,' said Clarissa.

Macleod made a grumpy face. 'You better have results with it,' he mumbled. He closed down the call. Clarissa saw Sabine was still on the call, looking bemused.

'Dining? We didn't eat anywhere. In fact, I haven't put any large receipts through. When we went up to Kylesku, we charged nothing expensive.'

'No, it's me. Do you know he bought breakfast for Hope?'

'McGrath, the murder detective?' said Sabine.

'Yes, and—'

'And we need to close this call,' said Patterson. 'She's just annoyed about it, okay? I need to go to bed, and she needs to fix up her clothing before tomorrow, because it's got torn. Let's get going and not spend the next hour discussing Macleod's breakfasting choices.' Patterson was gone with that outburst before Clarissa could say anything.

She wondered if he was getting annoyed with her. Maybe she'd been harping on about this too much. She was justified, wasn't she?

'I'm not going to bed,' said Sabine. 'I'm going to hit the gym. You want to come, Emmett?'

'No,' he said. 'I'm going home to read a good book. Catch everybody in the morning.'

The screen closed, and Clarissa shut her laptop. They were getting somewhere at last. Maybe she needed to keep things between Seoras and her at times. Patterson was saying a lot. She didn't mind the banter, but that last comment wasn't banter. He was making a point.

Clarissa thought about her previous roles. She was always under someone. There was always somebody above her who pulled her into line. She'd said a few things out of place in her career. She wasn't talking about when she spoke to the upper management and called them many things. The worst she had called someone was a bloody arsehole.

But she didn't regret that. Here she was saying things about Macleod. Yes, it was terribly tongue-in-cheek. Maybe she shouldn't be so forward in front of the others with it. Als would have told her off, probably. He worshipped Macleod. She turned and looked at her trews. Time to get the sewing done. Then she'd call Frank. Part of her just wanted to be home again. Still, it wouldn't be that long.

Chapter 13

Ferguson drove the car through Glasgow, aware that Emmett was speaking a lot more. It seemed to be the way with him. He said nothing until the cogs inside his brain got into gear. And then he just kept talking until he found out what he needed to know.

'Who's this Dudley then? Why do we call him the Grease?'

'Dudley's one of those people who knows things, Emmett. Without him, the underworld and the art world wouldn't meet together. Things would get in the way. Documents wouldn't be signed. You wouldn't have backgrounds to items, backgrounds that they didn't deserve. Some items, everybody knows the background, but it's not detailed properly. So certain documents arrive that make it look like it was detailed properly. Dudley can do jobs like that. But he also moves a lot of items around. He's got a large warehouse here in the middle of Glasgow.'

'So, not a good guy, then?'

'An irritating guy. Clarissa doesn't really remember him well, but Dudley remembers her. She tore him one when he tried to give her a certificate of authenticity for an item that was two centuries out from its correct date.'

'I can see she wouldn't appreciate that. She's very particular about her art. Forthright, from what I've heard. I've heard they call her Macleod's Rottweiler.'

Ferguson stared over for a moment and then looked out the window as she drove.

'I wouldn't remind her of that one. She doesn't take to it very well.'

'I'll bear that in mind, not that I was going to call her it in front of her. Whereabouts is the warehouse, then?'

'It's close to the river. Another couple of turns and we'll be there. Look around when you go in; see if you can spot anything. I'll do the same.'

Ferguson parked the car, and the tall blonde woman led Emmett into the rather dull-looking warehouse. It gave the appearance of a big shed from the outside, and once they'd stepped inside, it did nothing to change their opinions. Items weren't delicately laid out to be examined, rather, they were all just plonked here, there, and wherever. There was an occasional card with some of them, but Ferguson ignored those, preferring to make her own decision about what an item was.

'It's you,' said a voice suddenly from halfway across the warehouse. A small man scampered along.

'That's him,' said Ferguson to Emmett. 'I'll have a chat. No point in you listening in on this. See what you can find.'

Emmett turned away to examine the shed's contents. Douglas Dudley, in an open shirt with a medallion hanging down on a gold chain, approached the rather taller Ferguson.

'I'm here on official business, I'm afraid,' said Sabine.

The small man in front of her froze before he began spinning round, looking here and there within the warehouse. 'She's

111

not here, is she? Dear God, you haven't brought her.'

'No, I'm afraid not. DI Urquhart is elsewhere at the moment.'

'Oh, thank God for that. Last time—she just didn't stop. And she went round, in front of customers, ripping up my cards.'

'In fairness to my boss, she only ripped up the cards that were inaccurate.'

'She tore up seventy-five out of seventy-eight.'

'Well, start doing your research then. Although, I think she was more annoyed because it wasn't sloppy research. It was more inaccurate. Wilfully inaccurate.'

'As she's not here, we won't talk about it,' said Dudley suddenly. 'But what can we do for you? Item you want to buy?'

'I said "I'm here on business."'

'Well, I'm sure the art world and police headquarters can buy the odd item.'

'Tell me, what do you know about pieces MacPhail's bought?'

'Why do you bring him up?' asked Dudley. 'Don't usually deal with people like MacPhail. You know what he is, don't you?'

'I work with the police. I'm asking you a name. Of course, I've researched him.'

'Well, it would make sense then that I don't go near him.'

'So, you've not purchased anything for him? I mean, he's getting into the art world.'

'Is that what they call it? He's getting into something. Janice Smith, more like. Don't blame him for that. Present company excepted, she's one of the top women in the art world.'

'I assume you mean, from a professional basis, the identity of artworks and that,' said Sabine.

'That's what I said,' replied Dudley smoothly. 'Top woman,

like yourself.'

Sabine gazed at the man, and could see him grubbily hiding out behind a desk, magazine in hand, gawking at whatever woman was adorning the cover. He disgusted her really, and with good reason. Not just as a human being, but also with his rather banal love of art. He had a love of money, not of creative talent.

'Too hot for me, I wouldn't get involved with him. You make a mistake with that man and it's . . .' He made a motion with his hand across his neck. 'I've known a few dealers who have retired.'

'Disappeared off to sunnier climes?' asked Ferguson.

'Colder ones. Not a lot of sun beneath the ground.'

'You don't mind if I have a look around, do you?'

'This is an art warehouse. As long as you're buying, you can look wherever you want.'

Ferguson nodded, walked past the man, and found Emmett at the far side of the warehouse. He was being quiet again, hand rubbing his chin. He kept looking around at various items. Sabine clocked them immediately, but she waited for him.

'See some of these?' said Emmett. 'I mean, I know I'm no expert, but they look awfully familiar to some ones that were in the shop's catalogue.'

'They are very similar. They were moved on to MacPhail, weren't they?'

'Yes,' said Emmett. 'Has he said if he's dealing with MacPhail? Did you ask him?'

'I mentioned MacPhail, and he nearly went white,' said Ferguson. 'MacPhail's not someone the art world wants to be with. The art world is not as cutthroat, not so brutal. It is in the sense of bidding wars, false items, theft, and ownership. Maybe break a few teeth to get an item cheaper. All that sort of thing. Actually, disposing of people? No. True art world isn't like that. People like MacPhail getting involved in it causes a shudder in the usual art punters.'

'Do you believe him he wouldn't touch anything from MacPhail?'

'There's no way Dudley would. And having spoken to him it makes perfect sense. They call Dudley the grease, as you know. He's a mover and a shaker. He makes things happen for people. But often things can go wrong, people get annoyed, and if that happens, it's the man in the middle that usually takes the hit. Therefore, he doesn't deal with people he can't handle. He can't handle MacPhail.'

'Right then. So where did these come from?' asked Emmett.

'Let's go find out.' Sabine walked back across the warehouse to where Dudley was standing with a customer.

'This is almost seven hundred years old,' said Dudley. 'You can see by the line and the curvature that it comes from one of the top houses of the time. You can—' He paused.

Sabine was picking up the small white card that adorned the sculpture before her. The sculpture was about knee high. It looked good, in fairness. But it wasn't worth anything. In fact, it was made about five years ago. A blatant copy. Easy to pick out for someone like herself. She took the white card and in front of Dudley and his potential client, she ripped it up.

'What are you doing that for?' asked Dudley.

'The information on this card is not factual. It's incorrect.'

'What parts of it are incorrect?'

'Well, you dated it seven hundred years ago. This thing would be lucky to be older than a nephew of mine. He's ten.'

The couple who were talking to Dudley about the item, turned on their heels and left.

'You've been working with that woman for far too long.'

'Not been working with her long at all,' said Sabine. 'I don't agree with you doing what you're doing any more than she does.'

'True,' said Dudley. 'Well, I suppose it's better having you. You certainly look better.'

'That's rather rude,' said Emmett.

Ferguson looked down at Emmett, a small smile on her face. She saw he was deadly serious.

'Detective Inspector Urquhart is a woman in her later years. You can't expect her to have skin that's . . . less aged, such as DS Ferguson's. You need to see women in a different light.'

Dudley stared for a moment, as if Emmett was a unique object that he'd never seen before. Then he glanced up at Sabine. 'Is he for real?'

'More real than most of your antiques,' said Emmett smoothly. 'My colleague was talking to you about MacPhail. However, you said you had nothing to do with him. I've clocked at least five or six items, that we know were sold to MacPhail by Janice Smith.'

'Really?' queried Dudley. 'Because I didn't buy them from them.' Sabine stared at the man, wondering if this was a lie. But his hands were shaking.

'What's MacPhail doing in the market? Not good. The market's clean. Ferguson, you know that. The market's genuinely clean.'

'Well, you sell on a lot of stuff at over-inflated prices and you don't have the exact histories for them. Or rather, you lie through your teeth about them.'

'Yes, but it's clean,' countered Dudley. 'We don't fall out, we don't bicker in such a way that ends up with guns and fisticuffs and people in gutters. We don't do that. MacPhail does that.'

'And that worries you?'

'Of course, it worries me. If that's MacPhail's stuff, I want to know which is what. I need to shift it on.'

'Where'd you get it from?' asked Sabine.

'Well, you'll need to show me, because I don't know which is MacPhail's.'

Ferguson looked over at Emmett, but he gave a shake of his head and a nod back towards her, showing she should do it. Clearly, his skills were not as wonderful as he was purporting. Sabine took Dudley over for a walk amongst several items, pointing them out to him.

'I got these at Bradley's. You know?'

'The auction house outside Livingston?' asked Sabine.

'The very one. It's Bradley's. They're genuine, aren't they?'

Sabine stared at the various sculptures. 'Can you tell which is which? And who they're meant to be by? I think there's something not right about these,' said Sabine.

'Don't say that too loud. I've got customers in the warehouse,' said Dudley.

'About half of these are probably fake,' said Sabine indignantly. 'But these are good fakes. Not just good fakes. I can't be sure. Something's just not right with them. Something keeps bugging me about them. It's a wonder Bradley's didn't pick it up.'

'I can't speak for them. I deal with them a lot. They've got plenty of stuff coming through that I then sell on. But if they were all fakes, I wouldn't buy them.'

'No, you wouldn't,' said Sabine. 'You'd get them from another source.'

'These are gone, as of today,' said Dudley. 'And I'll be asking Bradley's about where they're getting MacPhail's pieces from.'

'No, you won't,' said Emmett. 'Not at least for the next four or five days. Not until we've asked them first.'

'Like hell. I could have bought plenty of other pieces during that time. I'm going to them today.'

'No, you're not,' said Emmett, 'because if you do, I will haul the rest of our colleagues down and we'll go through here and we'll lift every fake. We'll also charge you for what you're saying about the other items because you have no interest in them. You're mis-advertising your goods.'

'I take it back,' said Dudley. 'He's been spending time around the Urquhart woman.'

'I haven't even met the boss in person yet,' said Emmett; 'however I can bring her down if you don't keep your mouth shut.'

Sabine grinned, watching Dudley squirm. She knew that when she turned, he would watch her all the way out of the warehouse, so it was good for him to get a dose of medicine. Sabine turned, looked down at Emmett, whose face was emotionless. As they walked, she saw Emmett turn back and give a tutting noise towards Dudley.

'Turn round. I've already told you about that sort of thing. You don't get to stare at her. You really could do with some manners.'

Emmett started walking backwards towards the door, and his face, again, was emotionless. He was genuine in what he was doing. He wasn't just taking the mickey out of Dudley. Sabine was becoming fond of her colleague. For all that, he was strange. But it was a good strange. A pleasant strange, and seemingly, a strange that would stand up for you.

Chapter 14

The day was grey when they arrived in Montrose. The little green sports car had its hood up because of the rain that had fallen the whole way. Clarissa was in a bad mood because of this, and Patterson had kept quiet. He watched as she stepped out of the car, slamming the door behind her, looking around through the pouring rain for the front door of the chapel.

The building did nothing to lift spirits, for it was grey. With the sky so dark, you almost thought you were approaching it at night-time instead of in the middle of the afternoon. Patterson pulled his jacket around him, urging Clarissa to hurry, and then didn't wait for her as he spotted the large red door at the front of the chapel.

Approaching, he knocked on it briefly, then tried the door handle. When it opened, he stepped inside to a small vestibule with open doors into the chapel. He held the front door open as Clarissa ran through, closing it behind him. He looked around to see if anyone was there.

'Hello,' shouted Clarissa loudly. 'Anyone here? Have we got a priest or something?'

A man stepped through a door at the side, dressed in a priest's cassock. He had a large, bushy beard, but it was grey. Patterson thought he was around the same age as Clarissa. His eyes were soft, but they looked as if they could penetrate for all that.

'Well, I'm the priest,' said the man. 'You'll have to make do with me, because something isn't here.'

Patterson smiled but Clarissa scowled. 'I'm Detective Inspector Clarissa Urquhart and I'm soaked. Is there anywhere I can hang my shawl?'

The man appeared to rear slightly, taking in Clarissa's aspect, and then pointed to a hook just behind her. 'If you hang it there, it should dry. There are not that many warm places in here. What can I help you with?'

'Well, this is DC Eric Patterson and we're looking for someone. Someone whose Bible you signed.'

'You make me sound like some sort of superstar priest. I sign a lot of Bibles. We try to give them away, you see. It's a bit more like a loan.'

'I'm not interested in what you're doing,' said Clarissa. 'I'm interested in who you wrote this to. Her name was Cara Mackey.'

'Okay,' said the priest. 'Shall we go inside? We could probably find you a cup of tea.'

'I could kill for a coffee,' said Patterson.

'Probably best not doing that in here. We may be on holy ground, but it doesn't make you exempt from the law.'

Patterson smiled and followed the priest through, catching Clarissa's rather dirty look. She wasn't keen on this man who was quick on the take.

They sat down on a pew in the chapel and the priest disappeared for five minutes before coming back with a tray and some cups. 'I didn't have any milk. I don't use any myself, so I only have tea bags. I hope you're okay with black.'

'Have to do,' said Clarissa. 'Can you tell us anything about Cara Mackey, please?'

'You realise I'm a priest and I can't divulge anything that's been said in the confessional to me.'

'I realise that but Cara Mackey is missing. She had been living under a false name, See'am Moon, in Aberdeen. We found a Bible with your name in it, made out to Cara Mackey. So, we want to know why she's not using her real name. She may be in trouble.'

The priest nodded, but didn't look enthusiastic. 'You realise she's only, what, twenty maybe?'

'We are aware. We have a photograph of her,' said Patterson. He produced the image of the muse on his phone and the priest nodded.

'That's Cara. Cara was a troubled soul or rather, had a troubled upbringing. I met her several years ago. Her mother was struggling, really struggling. She had an alcoholic husband. She came home one day to find that he'd killed himself. Poor woman never got over that. Never knew how to cope with it. Went downhill quickly. She was dead six months later.

'Some say that people can die of broken hearts. This one was probably just smashed apart. She'd struggled with Cara. I think, with rejection issues when she was younger as well. The whole situation was just a mess. But Cara, she was put into foster care in the local area, so I kept the connection I had with them. She sought help here.

'I don't think the foster parents were bad with her. They just didn't make a connection. For some reason, she seemed to click with me. I never tried to push her into anything. Was there to talk. I did what I could to support her. The trouble with Cara was, and you can tell from the photograph, she really had the looks.'

'Stunning,' said Patterson.

'I think she came to talk to me because, well, I don't know. I think she thought I didn't have appetites in that way, being a priest and that.'

'Well, you're not meant to, are you?' said Clarissa. 'I mean, we know the history of the church and things have gone wrong, but you guys are not meant to seek a woman's company.'

'I think plenty of us have appetites like that,' said the priest. 'But we have them under control, most of us. We're a safe place for people to come to, or meant to be. And if there is a very good-looking eighteen-year-old girl, then that's exactly what we must be. But trust me, the appetites are there. We just don't indulge them. We don't bring them to the fore.'

'When she came for help, did it succeed? Was it any good for her?' asked Patterson.

'Because of her alcoholic father and her mother, Cara had been introduced to more of the darker side of life. She had contacts through her father to people who would have used Cara. Not in a good way. She had plenty of offers to use and sell her body. Of course, I cautioned her against that. She was struggling too, financially. Thankfully, she stuck with it. She became very devout.'

'What do you mean by that?' asked Patterson. 'It's got many connotations.'

'It does. She would attend our Bible studies, attend the church. She talked to me sometimes about the Maker and tried to help with certain church programs we were in. Cara tried to be part of our community. She would read that Bible, pray. She went to church camps. I think it kept her from being mistreated while she was growing up. I'm not sure the foster parents would have been able to stop her from going off the rails.'

'So, what happened then?' asked Clarissa.

'Well, she moved on,' said Father Kershaw, 'when she turned eighteen. She was interested in art, and frankly, she had an opportunity to work around art up in Aberdeen, and she went. I heard little from her after that.

'They say they will—they always do, don't we all—and then they don't. And those of us left behind get a little upset. But it's usually because they're excited, that they're making a new way, a fresh path. Our contact with people drops out when we don't see them, when we don't purposely think about them. I'd done what I'd done.

'I met her though, when I went to Aberdeen. Just along the street. She walked past and you don't miss Cara. The hair, the face. For a moment, I'll admit to this, I was quite taken. It was good having her around. It's funny, you take these vows, and I've stuck to them. I have been celibate. But sometimes it's just nice having good-looking people around you. A good-looking woman. I don't think there's anything wrong in that. You've got this good-looking man with you.'

Clarissa's face was stone. Patterson clocked the slightest twitch in her face but only the once.

'I indulged myself,' said the priest. 'I took her for coffee. In fact, I insisted she come to coffee with me. And we passed a pleasant hour and a half together, talking about old times, seeing how she got on. And I felt all the better for it. I'm not ashamed of it. It's just a fact of life.'

'Did she say much?'

'She said the art was going well. She showed me a photo of

a sculpture. Well, I could tell it was a sculpture of her right away. The feeling in it, the impression coming back at you, was Cara in that sculpture. Warmth, joy, happiness, a serenity. The piece, although the model had so little on, was not sexual. It was empathy; it was life: it was everything. It was Cara.'

'She was proud of it then?' asked Patterson.

'Deeply proud. She admitted to being the muse for the artist, but she wouldn't tell me who the artist was. I like art, but I'd never seen that artist, not seen his work. I know now that it's Ernesto Hunter, but that's because I did my homework. Found out what that piece was, and I saw several more pieces. I don't have money, but I know where some of those pieces are and where I can view them. And I have on occasion gone. Reminds me of a girl I cherished deeply. The warmth of a friend.

'But you say she's missing?'

'Some heavies from Glasgow were at her door. We entertained them as she ran off, but we're wondering where she's gone,' said Patterson.

'Well, if she comes here to this chapel, I'll obviously call you. However, she's not here.'

'Where else might she go?' asked Clarissa.

'The only thing I can think of is she might go back to her foster parents. Like I said, she didn't get on with them. She didn't click with them. But they treated her well. They were kind to her. Well, she vanished in a turbulent time and I think once she'd left, she probably appreciated just how good they were.'

'Would they be in contact with you? Would they have called if she'd come back to them?' asked Clarissa.

'They weren't religious people and didn't really see the church as being that beneficial for Cara. They talked about exams and stuff. And they were right, in a sense. She could have done with getting more exams and finding a better job. Or getting up and working in a museum. Wherever you arty types work.'

'Did she ever say things were difficult with the muse with Ernesto?' asked Patterson.

'She didn't tell me who he was,' said the priest. 'She indicated nothing about him directly. Only talked about the artwork. It wasn't like she was in love with a guy or anything. Distinctly not. Clara's funny like that. Now don't get me wrong, maybe one day it'll hit her. Maybe one day she'll be chasing after some guy. But she was about the artwork. She was about beauty and art. Never in my time with her did I see her hunger for a relationship, at least a sexual one. I think she wanted friendship. And in fact, that's what I had with her. Friendship.'

Clarissa put her tea down. Patterson noticed it hadn't been touched at all. 'Well, thank you for the information,' said Clarissa. 'I may contact you again, but if she shows up, please ring this number.'

She handed him a card with her details on it and they made their way back out to the vestibule. Clarissa put her shawl back on and Patterson opened the door. It was still raining outside.

'Is she streetwise?' asked Clarissa of Father Kershaw, 'would she be able to handle herself on the run?'

'Honestly, I doubt it. She'd head for somebody. She'd definitely make for somewhere she could hide out. Clarissa wasn't one for discomfort. She liked the trappings of a normal life, of a house, of heat.'

'Like I say, if she gets in contact,' emphasised Clarissa.

'Well, I hope you find her. It doesn't sound good.'

Clarissa pulled her shawl around her and marched off back to the little green sports car, Patterson following, and they climbed inside. Clarissa sighed and closed the door. Patterson turned to Clarissa.

'What a candid man. All that stuff about relationships and his feelings.'

'I don't get it—priests,' said Clarissa. 'Why on earth would they tell them they can't go off and be with someone? It will not stop them from doing their job, is it?'

'I don't know,' said Patterson. 'But something just made me think he was too candid.'

'Well,' said Clarissa, 'we need to get moving, then. Off to the foster parents.'

'Indeed,' said Patterson, but as the car drove away, he couldn't help but look back at the dull grey building. He thought back to the man with the grey beard, all dressed in black, probably now meditating or saying prayers.

Chapter 15

'I wouldn't ask,' said Emmett, 'but I think we might get in and find out what's really going on if we go down this route.'

Sabine eyed Emmett from across the room. 'It's a good plan,' she said. 'I'll do it. I'm not keen on wearing all that glamorous stuff. It's just not me.'

'And I wouldn't ask you to, but they'll be expecting it. If I'm going to play someone who's got a bit of money, I need to have somebody glamorous on my arm.'

Ferguson looked at Emmett. Would he ever look right with somebody glamorous on his arm? That was probably unfair. He was sitting in his chair, in the office, his delicately painted miniatures still sitting on top of the desk. He was a geek, wasn't he? They used that term with pride these days, the communities that participated in board gaming. That's what they called themselves.

'I'll need to pop downstairs. I've got a few outfits I could make up into something.'

'Take your time,' said Emmett. 'I'll go put a suit on, look a little more snappy. Not this old thing I walk around in.'

'Why do you wear a suit at work?' asked Ferguson.

'Because I was always facing the public, mainly. I was doing liaison. They didn't want us always dressed up in our uniform. So, you would go along but you had to look the part. I wore a suit. They didn't like jeans and a t-shirt. Apparently that didn't work well.'

'Up in Inverness there's a DI, Hope McGrath. She wears t-shirts mostly, jeans, boots.'

'Don't take this the wrong way,' said Emmett, 'but she could wear what she wants and none of those bosses would complain. I don't get that luxury. I'm not the renegade who looks terrific but the strange oddball on the side, who they've got here because he can do his job. You're fortunate, you're very fit physically, and you understand the art world. That's why you're here.'

Sabine went to turn away and leave the office, but there was a smile on her face. *He was warm, wasn't he? He was very honest, too honest sometimes, but didn't have a great view of himself. Was he overly attractive? No. He was one of those people you would just bypass in the street. But, did seem to be considerate, and that wasn't always a given round here.*

Sabine disappeared down to the female changing rooms, where she dug out a blouse, a snappy pair of trousers and a short suit jacket. She adjusted it, adding a bit of cleavage for show, and topped it off with a smart necklace. Her hair went underneath a broad-brimmed hat.

She clearly wasn't dressed for today's weather, which was raining, but then again, somebody hanging on to a man like Emmett was portraying, wouldn't be dressed for the Glasgow nonsense.

When she arrived back in the office, Emmett did nothing more than give an approving nod. He didn't try to wolf-whistle or butter her up. 'Spot on,' was all he said. He was wearing a suit that didn't fit him, but it looked expensive.

'Where did you get that one?' asked Sabine.

'Bit of undercover work I did previously; found it in the charity shop. It's cracking, I mean, it's really good stuff. Well-tailored, but it looks better if it doesn't quite suit me. It means I look like a man who's come into money, not one born with it.'

The pair left the office, and Emmett took them up the corridor. 'I asked about,' he said; 'we've got a top of the range BMW, belongs to one of the DCIs. He said I could borrow it for the afternoon. He insisted we don't go chasing people in it.'

'How do you get him to lend you that?'

'Well. He's not too hot on the computers. So, I got one of his other colleagues to set up this new range of apps for him. Apparently, he's quite pleased with it.'

'You're quite resourceful, aren't you?' said Sabine. She looked down at her colleague. He was a good six inches lower than her. And they looked a strange pair. But that was the point. He was a man who made his money by nefarious means. And he brought women along. They didn't go for them because of his looks. He had all the trappings to show off the money he earnt. He was spot on for the auction house.

Livingston lay between Glasgow and Edinburgh, and he pulled up in the commandeered BMW, parking it at the front door of Bradley's auction house in no particular place. As he stepped out, Emmett heard somebody shout over to him about where the parking bays were. He raised his hand, extending a middle finger, and heard somebody swear back at him. Sabine slunk her arm around his, and together they cruised into the auction house.

'Could you park your car properly, sir?' said a voice at the door.

'You can park it if you want,' said Emmett. He chucked the keys at the older man who gave Emmett a suspicious look.

'Who runs the place?' asked Emmett.

'Mr Bradley. I'm afraid Mr Bradley's out.'

Emmett took out a ten-pound note and tucked it into the pocket of the man speaking. 'Get me Mr Bradley, now.'

Emmett stood, Sabine's arm linked in his, and glared at everyone else who was watching him. Sabine did her best to take in the stares at her and try to show off her figure. It wasn't something she was comfortable with. Her figure was her figure, but she was playing the part, a woman who liked to be stared at and she was giving it her all.

'I'm Mr Bradley. Who are you?'

'My name's Docket, up from London. I think you've got some things that might interest some certain Saudi Arabian buyers of mine. They don't know what they're looking at, but it's got to look good. Somebody told me you had ways and means of acquiring the right thing.'

'Who said that?' asked Bradley.

'Well, we don't like to mention his name. Let's just say he's a friend of Janice.'

Bradley gave a nod. 'Come this way, Mr Docket,' he said. They were taken through into the main office of Mr Bradley who showed them to a sofa. He cracked open a bottle of whisky and handed Emmett a large glass full, before pouring one for Sabine too.

'Ice?' asked Bradley.

'Is it any good?' said Emmett. He stood up and looked at the bottle. 'Oh, we're not putting ice in this. This is the good stuff.'

'Absolutely,' said Bradley.

Bradley put the bottle down and turned away to his desk. Emmett instantly poured his drink out into a flowerpot, placed the glass down on the table hard, and then turned to Sabine.

'You don't need any of that. I'll take that one.'

He placed the drink down in front of him as Bradley turned back to look at him. 'What sort of things were you looking at? What sort of price range?'

'Saudi buyers. Top end stuff.'

'Small collectible pieces, lots of them,' whispered Sabine under her breath.

'Small collectible pieces, lots of them, but costing a bit. Of course, we'll ramp them up for the buyers. Doesn't have to be genuine,' said Emmett.

'Of course, it will not be genuine,' said Bradley. 'Not if it's going out of this country. Besides, they don't know what they're talking about. Especially new pieces. You can tell them anything.'

'You're a man speaking my language. What have you got?' asked Emmett.

'What do you need?'

'No following you,' said Emmett. 'You have stock, don't you?'

'Yes but what do your clients want? I can get them what they want.'

'That's going to take time though, isn't it? They're going to want it soon.'

'I can get them it soon, within three months,' said Bradley confidently.

'Some of what they want, I'm not even sure it's on the open market.'

'Doesn't matter,' said Bradley. 'I have a source.'

'Elsa, dear,' Emmett said to Sabine, 'You got your phone there? You have the list. Tell the man the sort of thing we want.'

Sabine pulled out her phone, pretended to click it on, and held it up in front of her. She rhymed off over twenty items made by different artists in varied years. There was nothing on the phone, instead, all dragged out of Sabine's head. Many of them cross-linked to what Janice had within her studio shop.

'I can do all of them,' said Bradley.

'This guy's good,' Sabine said to Emmett. 'I don't even know what half of these things are.'

'Are you sure you can get them?' asked Emmett.

'Of course,' said Bradley. 'MacPhail has a certain amount of clout. We'll get them for you. Contact me again in six weeks.'

'When do you need a down payment?'

'You pay on delivery. I don't mess about with this stuff. At the exchange, the money will be transferred. If it doesn't come through, I can always shift it somewhere else. It's in high demand. All the stuff I supply is in demand.'

'Very good,' said Emmett. He sat back, lifting the whisky. 'Do me a favour,' he said to Bradley. 'Why don't you take Elsa here round, tell her about a few of the objects out there. She can come back and tell me what she wants for her birthday. I don't mind if it's an expensive one.'

Sabine stood up, almost clapping her hands, looking like a woman who'd just been let out for the day. Bradley smoothly stepped over, put an arm around her, and she felt his hand on her hip, guiding her out the door. She wondered what Emmett would be up to in her absence, but she spent the next half an hour being told mainly lies about items in front of her.

Most of the items in the auction house didn't come up that often. She was amused at the number that were all together. She thought they'd be cleverer than that. Maybe they'd make them public one at a time or maybe they were just there for people coming in to order on demand. However, just like the pieces that Janice had, Bradley's pieces gave her an uncomfortable feeling.

He let her pick up any pieces she wanted, and she was careful not to examine them too closely. Instead, she would roll them around in her hands. Make a corny little joke about how this sculptor left this man naked or wasn't it all frolics on the way they sculpted them. She made sure she liked the animals as well, focusing on horses as a particular obsession of hers.

By the time they came back into the office, Bradley moved his hand off her hip and down to her backside. She sat down on the sofa beside Emmett, reached across and kissed him delicately on the cheek. Sabine was shocked when he turned, grabbed the side of her face and planted a proper, deeper kiss on her. He then sat back.

'Did she tell you what she wants.'

'I'll put it in with all the rest. You can have it. We're going to be doing enough business, I think.'

'Very good,' said Emmett, and stood up. Sabine joined him, noticing that Emmett's glass was empty, and she wondered which plant had been freshly doused in quality whisky.

'You can contact me on this number,' said Emmett, 'when you're ready.' He wrote a random mobile number, and then, with Sabine on his arm, left the building. His car arrived at the front door just as he stepped out, and the man he'd given a tenner to before handed him the keys. The door was held open for Sabine, and the pair embraced again before driving off.

As they took the BMW further out onto the ring road, Emmett pulled up at the local services. Sabine watched him as he began to pull sticker tape off the number plates, and the registration plate changed again. He got back into the car.

'Can't have them tracing down the DCI, can we?' said Emmett. 'I apologise for that kiss. I felt it was needed. Made sure that he knew I wasn't happy about the way he had his hand on your backside when you came back into the office. Sorry about that. You shouldn't have to deal with that.'

'It's fine, Emmett,' said Sabine. 'But thanks for asking. I'm perfectly okay. He's far from the roughest person I've had to deal with. Were you able to do anything while I was out there?'

'He's not daft. He left me in an office that has nothing of note sitting around. Wherever he keeps his key details, it's not there.'

'Well, he's just like Janice, so I think the items are being brought in. There's a lot of stuff there that doesn't come up for auction often. Too much stuff. And he won't be putting it all out together at once either, because if he did, people would notice. I smell a rat, Emmett. A big rat.'

'A MacPhail-sized rat. But why? What's it got to do with Ernesto, though?' said Emmett.

He drove back, parked up at the station, and Emmett dropped the keys back to the DCI he'd borrowed them from. When they got back into the office, Sabina had changed again, back into her comfortable trousers and neat blouse.

'Guess we should contact Clarissa. See what she wants us to do next. I think she'll be coming this way soon.'

'What were they doing today?' asked Emmett.

'They think they've tracked down the foster parents of our

muse Cara. They were going to see them. Funny, I thought I would have heard from them by now. But not so. Anyway. How about grabbing some dinner tonight? You and me. Just a buddy thing. You can tell me all about these games you play.'

'I would do. But I've got a session on tonight. Half-past six.'

'I could come and watch if you want,' said Sabine. 'Do you take any of your miniatures along?'

'You'll be bored out of your mind. You don't look like a board-game person to me, more of a gym person, aren't you? Maybe walks and stuff, or runs, or cycling.'

'You can try me, Emmett,' she said, 'try me and we'll see. But you have to come to the gym with me at some point. Try what I do, too.'

'Okay,' he said, 'That's a deal. I'll just go get this clobber off.' Emmett left the room, and Sabine reached over and picked up one miniature. It was a warrior woman with a leather warrior's outfit. She looked fearsome, and the sword she was carrying looked far bigger than her. *What was Emmett really like underneath all of this?* she thought. *He was quiet, but what went through his mind?* Sabine was keen to know her partner, because, unlike most of the men she met in these departments, he was very different.

135

Chapter 16

Clarissa parked the little green car and tutted at the rain again. She whipped her shawl around her. Part of it caught Patterson on the shoulder, but he ignored it, climbing out of the green car on his side. Quickly, they made their way down a small path that led to a semi-detached house. The garden on either side was neat, but as Clarissa studied the plants, she realised that none of them were anything fancy. All the bog-standard fare that you would pick up if you were at any half-decent garden centre. Patterson pressed the doorbell, and he stood in the rain, waiting.

'Harold, would you get that?' sounded a voice in the back of the house. Through the frosted glass, Clarissa saw a figure approach. Several locks were taken off, and then the door opened to a man who was well into his sixties, if not further on in life. He had a paunch belly and a neat cardigan that was zipped up at the front. Grey hairs came out of his ears, and he looked like he could do with a trim, but he had a jolly face and smiled at the pair of detectives.

'I'm looking for Mr and Mrs Smith,' said Clarissa.

'Well, that could be us. That is our name.'

'I'm DI Clarissa Urquhart. This is DC Eric Patterson. We

need to talk about Cara Mackey. I believe you fostered her.'

'Cara? All right. Can I see some identification?' said the man.

Clarissa pulled out her ID, showed it to the man, and he then stepped to one side.

'Come in,' he said, 'out of that rain. Go through to the lounge there. My wife's just tending to some plants out the back. Marigolds, I think she said, though she could have been referring to the gloves. I know little about these things. But Miriam . . .' He shouted, 'we got some detectives here to see us.'

The living room had a TV in the corner and a rather bland brown sofa. Around the room were photographs, many of teenagers and lots of the Smiths at various stages of their life.

'Have you fostered for long?' asked Clarissa.

'Can't have kids. So, when we couldn't, we decided we would foster. Give others a chance. Done it most of our lives. Given up now. Got too old. Kids are a handful. Cara was a proper handful.'

'Really? In what way?' asked Clarissa.

The door opened into the living room, suddenly causing everyone to look round, and a woman stood in an apron, holding a pair of scissors in one hand. 'Harold, you haven't even got them any tea. What have you been doing? Come on, out with you. Get out to that kitchen. Get the inspector over there something to eat as well. And as for this woman, she'll want something too, while she's taking her notes.'

Patterson nearly burst out laughing, but he held it together and watched to see how Clarissa would react.

'Hello,' said Clarissa, standing up. 'Sorry to intrude on you. I'm Detector Inspector Clarissa Urquhart, and the man taking

137

the notes over there would be Eric Patterson. He's a detective constable. Inspector ranks above constable.'

'Well, that's very modern,' said the woman. 'Harold. Tea!'

Harold disappeared out and Miriam sat down, taking off her apron, folding it neatly and placing it beside her chair. 'What are you speaking to us for, then?'

The statement was abrupt, but Clarissa didn't rise to it. 'We need to talk to you about Cara Mackey. Looking to get some background on her. Also, to see if you've spoken to her recently.'

'Cara,' said the woman. 'Cara was a handful.'

'Your husband said so,' said Patterson. 'In what way?'

'Bible Thumpers. Have you ever been around Bible Thumpers? Do you know the trouble we have had?'

'What do you mean?'

'There was a church down the road. One of these new ones. What do they call them? Harold,' she shouted. 'What do we call those ones down the road?'

'Call what?' shouted Harold from the kitchen.

'Those religious nuts down the road. What did you say about them? You said they were…'

'Happy clappies.'

'Yeah, they were happy clappies. Big drives out to the schools and that? Thought little of them. Built the kids up, offered them something and then left them. Kids made all these promises and stuff and then who's picking up the pieces? Not the happy clappies.'

'And Cara was into this, was she?'

'She was. Way too much. Very serious. Incredibly religious. Started having a go at us, telling us what we could and couldn't do. We'd never seen the like of it. She was only a teen. We're

138

not talking at the back end of teenage years either.'

Harold arrived with a tray and some tea in a pot, along with some China cups. He placed it down on a small table in the middle of the room and began to pour. 'Milk? Sugar?' He asked. Patterson nodded, and Harold made a cup for him and then gave Clarissa exactly what she wanted too.

'What's that shortbread, Harold?' asked Miriam.

'In the box from the back.'

'That's several days old. Get the fresh stuff, the one we haven't opened.'

'It's absolutely fine,' said Clarissa. 'We're not here to eat. We need to ask.'

'Harold, did you hear me?' said Miriam. Clarissa raised her eyes over at Patterson. He gave the most imperceptible shakes of the head.

'Can you tell me more about Cara?' asked Clarissa.

'Cara, she was so definitive. Black and white. You did something that upset her, that was it. You did something right. Oh, you were wonderful. She wasn't balanced. She—how would you say it?—wanted perfection in everything.'

Harold appeared with a tray of fingers of shortbread. He offered one to Clarissa who felt obliged to take it. Patterson took one too before Harold almost collapsed into a chair.

'Your wife said that Cara was very religious.'

'Happy clappies,' said Harold. 'The happy clappies got to her. They got all happy clappy together. I tell you, never seen the like.'

'Is that all it was, though? Just a passing fad?'

'Well, I thought so,' said Marion.

'No,' said Harold. 'She was too religious for her own good, but the thing was, she also liked the idea of perfection. She used to get the magazines, the girl magazines, the girly ones, the ones that told you how to look good and be beautiful.'

'Was she into all the makeup and that?' asked Clarissa.

'No. She more liked the concept of beauty, I think,' said Harold. 'She used to come and sit with me and ask me what I thought of different girls in the magazines. Very embarrassing. I mean, it's not the sort of thing you talk about, is it? Even if you were prone to looking. She was difficult to handle, you see. She'd go down to that happy clappy church but she wanted to copy the girls in the magazines and then some of the clothing wasn't appropriate. But by the time she was eighteen, she was more refined. She could highlight her figure without making it look like she was a tart, frankly,' said Harold.

'She looked like a tart sometimes. I was worried about the boys coming after her. Really was,' said Miriam.

'You said she was difficult to handle, though, in what way?' asked Patterson.

'Did what she wanted, and what she wanted was to be a model. At one point I had to stop her,' said Harold. 'I was quite shocked. Cara looks probably slightly older than she was. When she was sixteen, she thought she could just do whatever, and she replied to get into an art class.'

'What's wrong with doing art?' asked Clarissa.

'Everything's wrong with doing art,' said Miriam, 'when you want to be the sole object; she offered to pose in a nudes class.'

'Miriam found out and sent me along,' said Harold. 'I had to explain to the man there that he really should check IDs and driving licences before he employed anyone. Cara was a good-looking girl, but you need to be more thorough than that.'

Clarissa was finding the couple quite suffocating in some

140

ways but they did seem to have Cara's best interests at heart.

'Do you know Father Kershaw?' asked Clarissa.

'Father Kershaw, now,' said Harold, 'I had some correspondence with him because Cara had mentioned us and I think he was looking to understand her better. So, he wrote to us. He's not one of the happy clappies. One of the RC ones. You know, Catholics. Smells and bells, isn't it? Waving those incense things around. Bang, strike a gong for this, strike a gong for that. Still, he seemed more level-headed; said she was doing okay up in Aberdeen. Clearly still hadn't got rid of the religious thing, though.'

'Hadn't you found out about her? Asked about her up there.'

'No,' said Harold. 'She was eighteen now. Not for us to police her. Look, we didn't get on great. We got on. She was fed, she was clothed, she was looked after. But we didn't take to her pious nonsense coming at us. Although, like I say, when she got up towards eighteen she got rid of a lot of that.'

'Do you stay in contact with many of your foster children?'

'Quite a lot actually,' said Miriam. 'But like I say, Cara was not my favourite.'

'Would she come back to you guys?' said Patterson. 'If she was in trouble, would she run to you?' said Patterson.

'No,' said Harold. 'We'd make her face up to what she was dealing with. I was good and strict like that. You have to be, don't you? You have to understand. They need to deal with problems in life. Not just run away from them. Cara wanted an idyllic thing. She wanted to be drawn all day long. Photographed all day long. She loved that fashion feeling as a model.

'She came from a rough background,' said Miriam. 'Her mother, father, the issues they had, before passing on. Her

141

mother actually had her figure. I remember seeing a photograph of her once. Except it was damaged by drink and worry and whatever else. Fortunately, Cara didn't go that way. She wasn't big on the boyfriends either.'

'In what way? She lean a different way?' asked Patterson, 'or was she just simply not interested?'

'Not interested as far as I could see,' said Harold.

The conversation moseyed on, generally talking about how Cara was difficult to handle, and passing out plenty of theories from the Smiths about how to deal with a child like that. Eventually, Clarissa stood up, shook her hand to the couple, and made for the door. She got inside the little green sports car. She looked over at Patterson.

'Never ever let me say a word about my parents.'

'You never do,' said Patterson.

'No, and if I ever do, you just point me to those two. What are they like? That would have been hard work.' Clarissa drove off, and as she did so, Patterson noticed her staring in the rear-view mirror.

'What's up?' he asked.

'Somebody's just pulled up outside that house.'

Clarissa stopped and then she suddenly pulled the handbrake, spun the wheel, turned the car around, sending it shooting back down the road. The car which had dropped the men off had driven round the corner. There were several men at the door in suits similar to those that had been at Cara's back in Aberdeen. Harold was being dragged out of the house and thrown into the small garden. As Clarissa pulled up in the car, Patterson jumped out first, racing off ahead of her, while Clarissa reached down inside the car grabbing a small piece of wood.

Patterson entered the small driveway and was met by a young lad, slightly taller than him, with broad shoulders. Patterson dipped his shoulder underneath the man's swinging punch, driving the shoulder up into his stomach, and took him down in a rugby tackle.

Clarissa was coming up behind and watched as one assailant hammered Patterson and ran towards her. He had a knife in his hand and Clarissa spun the short stick out of her hand, low, just off the ground. It clipped him around the shins, caused the man to kick his own feet and he fell hard to the ground. He then felt a hard crack across his back of a nightstick before Clarissa spun it again to hit a third assailant across the face. She was pushed hard to the ground, her nightstick dropping. And it was then that she realised that the fourth man there was the one she'd bitten before.

'You ready for more?' she shouted. 'This time I'll bite the whole thing off.'

Patterson was back on his feet. It was with the help of Harold they pushed one assailant back. The nightstick was on the ground and Patterson picked it up, cracking it into the back of the legs of one assailant. This time, they looked around before the man who had been bitten the last time they met told him to get clear.

As he went to leave, Clarissa, prone on the ground, reached forward and grabbed his ankle, pulling him down. She dug her nails into his leg, and he shrieked. She went to stand up, the man's trouser leg rolled up and she could see her teeth marks from before. He reached down with his leg, kicking her, and she was forced to let go. Soon the four men had disappeared off, running round a corner where no doubt their car awaited.

Patterson called the incident in to the local station, asking for some back-up.

'Are you all right, Harold?' asked Miriam. 'Who were they? What were they doing?'

Clarissa sat up, her bottom now wet from the grass. 'I'm afraid to say these are the people after Cara. We're not one hundred per cent why.'

'Told you that girl was trouble. At least, it's your problem now.'

'I'm going to put a watch on you two,' said Clarissa. 'I'll make sure you don't get hassled anymore. Is there anything else you can tell me? Anything about who Cara could be in contact with? People like this.'

'We're respectable people,' said Miriam, helping her husband to his feet. 'We don't do these things.'

Clarissa believed that. After waiting for uniform to arrive, Eric left the Smiths with some of the local constables.

'Where are we going next?' said Patterson as they got into the car.

'Everywhere we go, somebody's roughhousing,' said Clarissa. 'We've got no better leads from our dynamic duo back in the house, nothing from Father Kershaw. I think it's time we went down to the city, spent some time there, find out what's really going on.'

'Fare-dos,' said Patterson.

'Maybe trace somebody with a large bite in his leg. Go on then,' she said. 'Make the joke.'

'I'm not going to make the joke,' said Patterson. He knew she wanted to mention being a Rottweiler, so she would punch him. But instead, he said nothing, and Clarissa almost thanked him for it.

'Long drive though,' she said to Patterson. 'Strap yourself

144

in.' Before he made a click with the seatbelt.' He found himself pushed back into the car. It wouldn't be long really, would it?

Chapter 17

It was still raining when the little green car pulled into Glasgow that evening. More of the station lights were still on than would have been at Inverness. Glasgow and Inverness were both obviously twenty-four-hour stations. Being a larger city with more than one station, Glasgow always felt busy. This was probably why Clarissa was happy enough being up in Inverness.

She had called ahead to the team, saying she wanted to meet that night. However, she had discovered they were not in the office. A message was sent advising them to come back in, for she would arrive sometime around half past ten.

It had taken longer than she suspected to sort out Uniform, with the problems at the Smiths. They wanted statements; they wanted guarantees of safety, asking who was involved. All Clarissa wanted was to make sure that there was some sort of protection put on for them. She'd even called Macleod, but all he told her was at her sort of level, she should be able to deal with that.

She asked if he wanted to get involved with the meeting that night, but Macleod said no. He had something else coming up that he was dealing with and told her she'd have to get this going on her own. He was available but he felt he wouldn't be for long. She tried to ask what was going on, but he couldn't say. It was all a bit strange.

Feeling slightly discombobulated, she parked the car up at the Glasgow station and climbed the steps up to the office of Sabine Ferguson. When she arrived, Sabine was there, as was Emmett, her new detective sergeant. Macleod had acquired him from somewhere else, didn't know how long he was going to stay, and didn't know what else he was going to do with him. Emmett had been rather like Clarissa. Nobody had wanted her. Nobody had wanted him. But his was a demeanour thing. It was the fact that he struggled sometimes to play with people. She was a hothead, and she knew it. Still, that was everyone else's problem, wasn't it? Not hers.

Patterson entered the office behind Clarissa, stepped beyond her and shook hands with Ferguson, before turning to Emmett Grump. He shook the man's hand, welcoming him to the team. Emmett was sitting in a T-shirt, which Clarissa was rather bemused by. It appeared to have some sort of potato figure with what she could only imagine was one of those lightsabre things from that science fiction movie. The t-shirt made little sense to her but Emmett smiled as he saw her looking at it.

'It's a good one, that, isn't it?' he said. 'Made me laugh.'

Clarissa also turned to look at Sabine, who was smiling, in her jeans, along with a checked shirt worn over a crop top. She seemed in excellent form despite what had been going on recently, and Sabine offered her chair to Clarissa. They could have taken a formal meeting room, but Clarissa liked to keep things within her own area and this part of this Glasgow station was the Arts Department.

'Right then,' said Clarissa. 'Let's see what we've got. What have you two been up to?'

Sabine filled in the detail about the visit to the auction house, including a rather great portrayal by Emmett. She told Clarissa about the art pieces, her reservations about whether they were genuine; reservations that were growing every time she thought about the pieces. Emmett explained he thought pieces were being moved.

'It looks to me like Janice Stewart is getting the items from somewhere. MacPhail may be supplying them,' he said, 'sending them out to reputable places. Some of them know what's coming. Maybe others don't, and they are being passed off as genuine. Sabine said there were too many pieces there that don't come up for auction that often.'

'It was like a condensed antiques roadshow on TV,' said Sabine. 'It was crazy. It's like that bit they do on the telly. They have a whole day of it, most of it pretty low key. But the television half hour has everything. Well, that's what the showroom was like. A showroom of the half hour off the telly! You don't see that many excellent pieces available at once. You know it's not right, Clarissa.'

Clarissa thought for a moment. 'Good work, you two,' she said. 'But they're doing it for what reason?'

'Money, I assume,' said Emmett. 'I assume that they're getting these made cheap, and then flogging them off as something else. He was quite happy, Bradley, to tell me they weren't the real thing. We were going to make money off them. He's obviously looking for a cut of that. Well, it seems like everybody's getting fatter from the pot, and MacPhail's in the middle of this. He's seen it as a good thing. He's probably still going with Janice. It would make sense. Keep her close, especially as it's a new venture for him.'

'But he's not money laundering with it,' said Sabine. 'He's just making money, I think.'

'Well, we've had a heck of a time hunting down Cara. Still haven't done it yet and kind of run into a dead end. So, what's the play then?' asked Patterson. 'What do we do?'

'You were desperate to come back here to Glasgow,' said Sabine to Clarissa. 'Are you here to shake things up? Do we march in and talk to MacPhail about it?'

'We can't do,' said Clarissa. 'We don't want him to know we're onto him. Two people are missing, Ernesto and Cara. I don't know if MacPhail's got them or not, but we can't risk it. We can't risk him ending up cutting and running. He's more than likely to just kill them, dispose of them, and cut his losses if he thinks we're onto him.'

'So, what do we do then?' asked Patterson.

'Why don't we conduct a stake out,' said Emmett. 'It could be a good three-month operation here, watching everything going on. We know Janice's place, we know Bradley's, but we could soon find out where else Janice is sending stuff off to. We may track it back to MacPhail.'

'Well, this could be big, dammit. We could have him banged to rights,' said Sabine. 'We wouldn't be lifting him for the murders and the prostitution rings and everything else that he's involved in, but we'd be lifting him for something. This station would be singing and dancing our praises.'

'No,' said Clarissa, 'still two people at his mercy, potentially. I won't sacrifice them just to haul in a big fish.'

'So, what do we do?' repeated Patterson.

Clarissa stood up and walked across towards Emmett's table. She was looking out at a cityscape of lights. Her hand absentmindedly went down to the table. She felt it knock something over. Looking down, she picked up what looked like a miniature gorgon?

'What are these doing here?' she asked.

'Don't mind them,' said Emmett. 'It's just my stuff. When I'm bored, it's what I do. Helps the mind take over.'

Clarissa looked at the hideous figure looking back at her. It was well painted, in fairness. It looked like there was some sort of undercoat to bring the colour out.

'Why have you got these?' said Clarissa. She thought about saying nothing but she couldn't stop herself from asking that question.

'It's what I do. We were out tonight. Playing games,' Emmett said. 'Sabine quite enjoyed it.'

Clarissa looked round at her. 'You were playing games?'

'Like a board game. Got some of his figures, though,' said Sabine. 'I'm not sure I understood fully what was going on, but it was fun. Friendly bunch of people.'

'I'm glad to see he's getting on so well but the big dog's in town,' said Clarissa. 'There'll be no more gaming for a while. We're going to go on a stakeout. But when we stake out, it'll be an active one.'

Patterson's head rolled backwards. 'Don't you even think about doing that, Pats; you need to be on the ball.'

'What do you mean by an active one?' said Sabine.

'She means that we're going to stake out Janice's. Then we're going to follow wherever these vehicles go, only we're really going to follow them,' said Patterson. 'It will not be a three-month tea and sandwiches job. She's going to want everywhere they're going in the books by the end of the night.'

'Darn right we will. I told you, we've got two people missing. That's got to be the priority. Now, this whole racket that they're running, it's just helping us find out if Ernesto and Cara have been grabbed by MacPhail. They may not have. They may just want them. We have got no definite link between MacPhail and them. Need something concrete, something we can hold up in court.'

'We need to be careful,' said Sabine. 'Macleod warned us.'

'He did. And we have been careful, and Patterson and I have been attacked twice.'

'That's not good,' said Sabine.

'No it's not, and it's partly why I'm here. Because frankly, I want protection, and not from Pats.'

'Aye,' said Patterson. 'What do you mean by that? Anyway, you don't need protection. You bit the guy on the leg.'

'You bit a man on the leg?' said Emmett. He had been sitting back, thoughtfully, until this comment was made.

'He was trying to kill me,' said Clarissa. 'That's my defence.'

'Well, then we'd better be careful. I'm not the greatest at these sort of things.'

'And you haven't worked with us before,' said Clarissa. 'Sabine, Patterson, and I will do it. We are used to working together. Three should be more than enough to cover it. You can, well, I don't know,' said Clarissa.

'I'll start doing some digging, see if we can find Cara, see if I can find more of the links; see what's happening with where the artwork is moving to. When I was in the Livingstone warehouse, Bradley's place, I realised that paperwork still has to be generated, even if it's just to cover what had come in. Things move about, you fill them in, you move the good stuff out of the way quickly. But you still have to fill in what's going on, then they'll do it,' said Emmett. 'Somebody like MacPhail will have this covered. It won't be left to a "Oh, we stuck it in the back of the van and went for it."'

'So we take Stewart's studio,' said Clarissa. 'That's where we move first, and we see what she's up to. Once we've that done, we see where the vans go to, where the stuff gets delivered, and we stake out those places.'

'I'm off to find us a hotel,' said Patterson. 'We'll get on to planning tomorrow morning.'

'Be in here at nine o'clock.' said Clarissa. 'We look at Janice's studio. First thing tomorrow; it'll be a twenty-four-hour surveillance. We'll need you to run food supplies and all the rest of it, Emmett.'

'He's quite an accomplished actor,' said Sabine. 'When we got into the warehouse and indeed even back at the Janice's studio, he knew what he was doing.'

'Thank you,' said Emmett, rather shyly. 'I'm just following Sabine's lead.'

'Well, it's all congratulations and happy slapping on the back. The big dog's in town so we get after this tomorrow. We push this investigation on and get ourselves a resolution. No more pussyfootin' about. We're going after it. I need to find these two people.'

'And I need to find a bed for the night,' said Patterson, leaving the room. Sabine could hear him outside on his mobile phone and waited until he came back in and told Clarissa where they were staying.

'Welcome, Emmett,' said Clarissa, shaking Emmett's hand. 'I don't know what these little figures are on your desk or know why you find it so enjoyable. Each to their own.'

'In fairness,' said Emmett, 'You don't know what these little figures are on my desk. I don't know why you wear those tartan trews. Or that shawl.'

152

'Style, my dear,' said Clarissa. 'Style. Something your T-shirt says you don't have. Sorry. No offence,' she said.

'None taken,' said Emmett, and watched her disappear out of the room with Patterson. He then turned and looked at Sabine.

'Guess that's our night, then. It's a pity. You were going well in that game. I was hoping I could show you a few more moves. You had a couple of unlucky dice rolls.'

'It was fun,' said Sabine. 'Would they still be playing?'

'Some nights they'll go on till one or two in the morning. If the games are good.'

'Grab your jacket,' said Sabine. 'I'm game if you are.'

'Well, I've never missed beating up David's half-arsed goblin team, so let's go and do it.'

Sabine wasn't sure what half-arsed goblin team Emmett was talking about. All she knew, it was her team seemed to be giant rats. Still, it had been fun. And fun was something Sabine needed because the world was all too serious.

'I'll be down in the car,' she said. 'Knock the lights off.'

'Will do,' said Emmett. As they left the office, Sabine heard a comment under a constable's breath, talking about the t-shirt that Emmett was wearing.

'Did you hear that?' she said.

'Yeah,' said Emmett. 'They're wrong, though. I'm not that way inclined. Why someone would be that way inclined simply because they wear a t-shirt like this? Makes little sense.'

'Did you fit in at the last place you worked in it?' she asked.

'Not really. Not really fitted in anywhere. Gotta be honest, Sabine; you're the first person to come out and play my board games with me.'

'Let's go play some more,' she said. Together, they walked

153

down to the car. Sabine felt a certain fondness for the man who sat with her as she drove out to one of his friend's houses. It was funny what life threw up. It was certainly easier than working with Clarissa. *Poor old Patterson,* she thought. *He carries it well. But that woman can be hard work some days.*

Chapter 18

The following morning, the arts team had gathered again at the police station, making plans to stake out Stewart's studio. It took most of the day to coordinate cars, times, and allow everyone to have a break for round-the-clock surveillance. Emmett wasn't doing the hands-on surveillance; instead, he would bring supplies and work on any matters that came up from their observations.

By late that night, it was Sabine and Clarissa who were sitting inside a car across the road from Janice Stewart's studio. There seemed to be the theme to the weather, for the rain was still pouring down. They weren't in Clarissa's little green car, which would stand out far too much for what they wanted to do. Instead, they sat in a rather bland Vauxhall.

'So, what's the deal with Emmett then?' asked Clarissa.

'What do you mean, "What's the deal with Emmett?"'

'Well, you went off playing his games with his little figures.'

'I'm just being friendly,' said Sabine.

'I wasn't suggesting anything else, just asking what's the deal with him? I wasn't making out you were some sort of item. Seemed that way, though; with that t-shirt he had on, why would anyone fall for him?'

Sabine bit her lip. She hated this. They always had a go—the guys looking at her and all they ever wanted was her figure. Yet the man didn't have a figure, and there was Clarissa having a go at him for it. Sabine guessed all women were different too.

'He's just a board gamer; that's what he does. He's got a nice little community of friends who seem to get on. It's actually quite fun. He was explaining it all to me, helping me out while we were playing the game, because a lot of it was going over my head. It takes a lot of time to play those games, you know.'

'I'd probably be more of a cards' person. Try to decide if you're bluffing or not. What do you call it? Vingt-et-un? Twenty-one? That's the one, isn't it? Make sure it adds up to twenty-one and doesn't go over. Well, I could just about manage that,' said Clarissa. 'Frank likes cards. Sometimes play them with him.'

'There's not a lot happening at the studio, though, is there?' said Sabine.

'Not really,' said Clarissa. 'Oh, look. They seem to be shutting up shop for the night.'

It was around ten o'clock, and Janice was leaving. As soon as she'd walked along the street, Clarissa made her way over in the rain and peered in through the window. Sabine sat in the car watching her.

Clarissa had been desperate to have a look in, to confirm Sabine's suspicions, but there had always been somebody in the studio; someone who may identify her. The lilac hair, the tartan trews and the shawl kind of gave her away.

As Clarissa got back into the car, she gave herself a shake, half soaking Sabine. She turned to the taller woman. 'You weren't kidding me on, were you?'

'I told you,' said Sabine.

'I mean, they must be having a laugh. Some of those are not real. There's one item there—I don't think I've ever seen the real thing. And I know for a fact that it's not real for the genuine piece disappeared underground. If it came back up, it would not sit in a place like that for easy buying. It would come out at a proper price. Our MacPhail's not that sharp on it.'

'Or Janice,' said Sabine. 'She'll be the one advising, surely.'

'I guess there's not much else to do,' said Clarissa.

'I thought we were watching it through the night.'

'For what? It's fully loaded up, isn't it.aren't we? All those shelves are full.'

'Maybe it comes in one burst and that's just what's in the studio. Maybe the real things come through at night and get transferred out.'

'All right. I won't be known as a boss who didn't take my shift. We'll sit here. What time's Patterson taking over from me, anyway?' asked Clarissa.

'Two.'

'Bloody two,' said Clarissa. 'That's four more hours. Do you realise that? Four more hours till I get to my bed. Maybe I'll phone Frank. He'll still be up. If I wait much longer, he won't be.'

'Great,' said Sabine. 'But do you really want to talk away about stuff in front of me?'

'Why don't you get out and go for a wander,' said Clarissa. 'You need to stretch the legs anyway, especially your legs. They're longer than mine.'

Sabine didn't argue with that. She was in a good mood, too. They were moving forward in the case, and she'd had a good night out last night with Emmett. She found him fun, in a rather subdued way. Pushed nothing on to her. Never tried to get her to do anything she didn't want to do. Introduced her to his friends and let her get on with it.

Sabine had trouble as a tall woman. A lot of men felt intimidated by her, felt they had to big themselves up. She'd done without a boyfriend for the last while. That was just as well. Work had been busy, running the Glasgow office with Clarissa all the way up in Inverness. She'd spent a lot of time on her own. A lot with training on top of that, doing her running. She was looking forward to getting Emmett into the gym, although he might not be as keen. She wondered if he would be up for a bit of light boxing.

Sabine crossed the road and cut down an alleyway round the back of the studio. She noted the shuttered doors as she wandered down the passageway, which was big enough for a lorry to get down. She looked up and around her.

Glasgow in the rain could be pretty depressing. Like anywhere, when the sun was out, it was great. But she understood why they had their sense of humour. The banter. Anything to have a laugh when the weather came in like this. After all it was the west coast of Scotland.

She heard a lorry turn round the corner at the far end of the alleyway. It was coming along, but by the time the lights had fully lit up the alleyway, Sabine had manoeuvred herself into an opening by a locked door. She'd stay here until it went past.

As she waited, she wondered just what was going on in that studio. She remembered Clarissa's words; it would be an active stakeout. She always found her boss to be slightly chaotic. Sabine was a more reserved person. Yes, she could handle herself. Yes, she could be dynamic when she wanted to be.

Sabine was a dynamic person who also enjoyed quiet time, reflection. She would run her guts out and then sit down with her smoothie, looking at a river, the countryside, somewhere, the sea maybe—anything to take her mind off life.

Here, she was now stuck in a doorway, waiting for a van to go past, but she was happy. And then the van didn't go past. She leaned out carefully. The lights of the van were switched off now, and she saw a dark figure approach what she thought was the rear of the studio. Shutters went up, and there was a mumbling between two men.

'We're late. They'll be here for delivery soon. She wasn't happy on the phone. If MacPhail finds out . . .'

'Don't mention his name when we're out here,' said a second voice. 'Told you that before.'

Sabine peered again, and she watched as several boxes were loaded into the rear of the studio. She picked out her phone, making sure it was well hidden in the doorway, and texted Clarissa.

'Keep watching' was the response and Sabine did so, wondering if Clarissa would wait in the car to follow the lorry. Another message followed, saying she was bringing Patterson in. Sabine watched as the two men finished unloading their lorry. The lights of the wagon came on again, and Sabine made herself as small as possible within the alleyway. The lorry went past without noticing her, and Sabine walked round, looking at the rear of the studio.

The shutter was unlocked. She was sure previously in the day, when she'd passed by, there'd been a lock on it, but now it was left open. Indeed the lock was at the side.

Slowly, Sabine went to lift the metal grills that now protected the shop, even though the shutter was unlocked. As she lifted it up and heard a faint rattling, someone touched her behind. She spun instantly and almost lashed out a punch until she saw the lilac-coloured hair.

'You could have told me you were coming round.'

'What are you doing?' asked Clarissa.

'The stuff's in there. I was going to see what it was. Shutter's unlocked.'

'Then they must be leaving it for someone. You don't bring stuff in like that and forget to lock up.'

'We'll need to be quick then,' said Sabine. She continued pushing the shutter up, and Clarissa made her way into the darkness inside.

'You're not going to believe this,' she said.

'What?' asked Sabine.

'These, they're fake.'

Sabine looked past the shutter and saw that Clarissa now had a pen torch out and was examining various figures in boxes.

'These aren't the real deal. It's minor. It's very minor. I know some experts that would miss this. But what you're feeling was right. These are fakes. These are being made and then sold off as originals. Bradley must be auctioning them out. MacPhail is making money off this.'

'The shelves are all full inside. You think these are—'

'These are going out tonight,' said Clarissa, 'it's why it's left open at the back. Somebody's going to come and get them. I need to get back outside quick,' she said.

Sabine saw the woman working quickly, packaging everything back up. And when she stood back outside, Sabine pushed the roller shutter door back down. They hadn't moved the lock, still left off to one side.

They could hear a truck close by now, though, above the

constant Glasgow noise. In the distance, there were police sirens. The city was alive, but this sound was closer. Sabine dived back into her little alcove and watched as Clarissa raced to the other side of the street. She slung herself up and over a wire gate, landing on the other side with an oof.

Sabine couldn't see her after that and wondered where the woman was. As the truck flooded the alleyway with light, no one could be seen. More men got out of this truck, and the shutter door went up quickly. These men looked to be more astute.

Sabine held her ground, only peering round carefully. She saw the black figures disappearing back in and out, and they never put a light on in the shop once. The back door of the wagon was open. When Sabine peered out and saw both men go into the shop, she also saw a black figure haul itself over a wire gate, and then rush towards the van.

Two men came back out, but they kept going back and forward, putting more boxes in, until eventually they locked up again. Sabine looked down at her phone. There was no message, nothing. Clarissa had gone round the back of the truck, maybe to fire off a quick photograph. *Where was Clarissa now? In the street?* Sabine couldn't think too hard on this, for the truck was on the move.

Carefully, Sabine hid, letting the truck slide past. The rear of it was locked up tight and once it had left the alleyway, Sabine removed herself fully, stepping back out into the rain. She scanned the alleyway, looking to see where Clarissa was. But she saw a figure at the end. It was in shadow, but she reckoned the height was correct, and started walking towards it. It came towards her at pace.

'Patterson,' she said. 'Did you see that?'

'I saw the operation. Saw some of it,' he said. 'I was in my car, and then Clarissa texted me, told me to come and have a look.'

'Did you clock a reg?' asked Sabine. Patterson nodded, and they both rhymed it off together.

'Good. Now let's go follow it.'

'Where's the boss?' asked Patterson.

'She was over this fence here, but she ran round the back of the wagon. Did you see her?'

'No, I might not have been here.'

'She must have been hiding somewhere else.'

Rather than shout out loud, Sabine took her phone, sending a text to Clarissa, asking where she was.

'They looked like right hoods, those two. Knew what they were doing,' said Patterson. 'The driver certainly had a gun tucked in his back pocket. It was a good job we didn't engage them. If they're armed, we might have to call in a response unit.'

'Indeed. And we might have to call in the search unit to find this boss of ours. I mean, where is she?'

There was a a vibration on Sabine's phone. She held it up, the light burning into her eyes, as she read the quick message. 'On the truck. Follow it.'

'No,' said Patterson. 'You're kidding me.'

'She did say it would be an active surveillance.'

'I know,' said Patterson, 'but I reckon those are MacPhail's men. If they get her on there, they'll just kill her. What is she doing?'

Doing what she always does, thought Sabine. *Charging in. Solving it.* But she wasn't happy about it. Together, the two of them sprinted for the car.

162

Chapter 19

The truck rumbled along, causing Clarissa to hold her hands out, bracing herself on either side. It was dark inside, but she gradually took out her mobile phone and switched on its flashlight. She could peer out from behind the box she'd crouched behind. It was right at the rear of the van, the back of the loading section, and she could hear the cab just beyond her.

The men inside weren't saying much. No directions were given, but occasionally they'd mutter something indistinct. With the flashlight on, Clarissa looked around the interior. There was a large assortment of crates and boxes. In fact, she was truly staggered by the amount being shipped around. She looked down at her phone. There was a text from Patterson.

'Bless you, Pats,' said Clarissa. *He's worried about me. I've been doing this longer than he's been living.* She wasn't far wrong. She had, in fact, been a police officer before Pats was born. Just. But it was true. She'd been in many a sticky situation and she'd always had the guile to get out of it. And when that didn't happen, well, you just bloody well made sure it worked. Sometimes you forced the issue.

The van turned round a corner and Clarissa was shifted

across, hitting her shoulder on the interior wall of the lorry. She stifled a moan as the van stopped. She crouched down behind the crates again. The rear doors flung open.

'I hope you've loaded these correctly.'

'Last stops at the back. This stops at the front. Look, it's marked up, okay?'

'How is it marked up? There are no labels on it.'

'It's just got the initials, hasn't it? This one, BB.'

'Bethula Bazaar. Yeah, you're not daft, are you? Come on then, get a crack on. We need to get this done before we see the sun. You know the boss gets mad if we're not back on time.'

Clarissa heard large crates being lifted and thought to herself, *Bethula Bazaar.* It was a colloquial name for an antique merchant. She made a note of it on her phone, texting the result to Patterson.

'We know where you are. We're following you. Get out of the van,' came the reply.

The message sent was simple. But she would not listen to Pats. Besides, if they were following her, Sabine was there. She knew how to handle herself if things got rough. It was the reason Clarissa had her on the team.

Clarissa hid down again as the rear door closed and she was plunged into darkness. She flicked on the light of the mobile phone, finding it somewhat comforting. This time, she sat down on her bottom. It would be easier than trying to balance, as the lorry pitched this way and that. Not that big a lorry, one of the seven and a half tonne ones.

She could legally drive it, even though she'd never driven one in her life. One oddity of the old driving licence, nowadays. The youngsters didn't get the same. Plus, she was also legal to drive a minibus, something else she'd never driven.

Well, she thought, *maybe they just knew the value of people back then. Had a bit more of a trust in them.*

It was another fifteen minutes before the lorry stopped again. Out they got out and opened the rear doors, Clarissa snuck a peek. The men were wearing hoodies, pulled up, but they didn't have masks on. Clearly, they didn't want to be seen as doing something illicit and make it completely obvious. However, it was obvious. It was the middle of the night, and they were dropping items off to antique dealers, and possibly auction houses.

'You've got a chance to get out,' came the text message. 'Take it.'

Pats was getting into a less confrontational mode now, trying to urge her out. But the important thing was that Clarissa remained on board to see where the van went. She'd take the chance. More importantly, maybe they'd go via MacPhail's. Find something that would tie MacPhail in directly. If Clarissa was there, she could take photographs. In fact, she should take photographs of what the men were doing.

The light on her phone was off. She peeked up over the top of the boxes, firing off a few shots. Then she brought her phone back down. There were no men in the picture, just the tops of boxes. She'd have to try again. She went to, but suddenly the rear doors were closed, and she was back in darkness.

This was frustrating. Very frustrating. But it dawned on Clarissa that something else was in play here now. Every time they stopped off, the men would come closer to her. The boxes between her and them were rapidly being taken away. How many stops could they have? Four? Five? Six? They weren't quite over halfway after the first two stops, so maybe five or six.

She'd have to get out soon, but it would be harder the longer she stayed. After all, they'd be coming right inside. They'd spend more time in the lorry unloading than they were doing previously. She'd have to really hotfoot it out of there. She couldn't very well pretend she got trapped in and play the little old lady act.

'Time to get out.' This was Ferguson, now texting her. Ferguson didn't offer advice the way Patterson did. She was more restrained and probably trusted Clarissa more. That may have been because she didn't work with her, whereas Patterson was used to being around her and having Clarissa charging about.

But this was different. She was working now and working well. Ten minutes later, the rear of the doors opened again on the lorry, and Clarissa put her phone up above. This time the photographs came back with the top of hoodies, and Clarissa sat down again.

'Taking a lot of load through here today,' said a voice,

'Yeah, we didn't drop here last time, did we? I heard they had a row with our boss, but they've paid a bit of money and, well, I'm not sure their nose is in too good a shape. I think that's what happened. Were you there?'

'No, and if I was, you know I wouldn't talk about it, anyway.'

'Come on, get moving. I don't care if there's a lot of stuff. We need to get it offloaded in the ten minutes he allows us.'

'Damn right, ten minutes.'

When the door shut this time, Clarissa put on the light of the phone. She looked around at the boxes before her. *Two stops maximum*, she thought. She texted Patterson. 'Two stops, Pats. Only two stops left. You might need to make a diversion for me.'

'When?' came the reply.

'Not this one,' texted Clarissa. 'The one after. We do it then. Give me something to get out.'

'It's a good job we're in pursuit then, isn't it?' said Pats. 'What would you have done if we had lost the wagon?'

It was typical of him, thought Clarissa. *He needs to stop pointing out his boss's failings.* 'But you didn't,' she texted back. 'You see, I have trust in you. Make that diversion.'

Clarissa opened one box near her and in the torchlight from her phone, she looked at the piece before her. *Incredible*, she thought. *Somebody was turning their hand into making a Chambers. And it was very, very good. But this piece wasn't available at the moment. This piece was believed to be in the archives. The collection of a certain Swiss artist taken for him by a certain female thief who hadn't been captured by the European authorities. My sources said it was the artist who had gained the piece, kept it away, never to be brought out. Somebody was going to flog this, and it would make an absolute fortune. It was good, very good. It could have fooled me, except I know where the piece currently is.'*

Once again, the truck pulled up, and this time, Clarissa didn't put her phone over the top to take photographs; the men were too close. By the time they'd finished, there were only three boxes left, Clarissa hiding behind a large one that would require two men to carry.

She could feel the tension beginning to rise now and reached up inside her shawl. She had a nightstick in there, a small retractable one, brought with her because Macleod had called it, saying what MacPhail was and the dangers of investigating him.

Well, she wouldn't be caught out. The next time the truck

stopped, Clarissa wasn't on her bottom, but crouched down on her haunches. She heard the back doors open. The two men came in. The box she was behind was large enough to cover her, and provided they didn't take it first, she'd be okay. She couldn't trust them to do that, and so the nightstick was out in her hand, still retracted, but ready to be sprung out.

'Get the big one last,' said one man, and Clarissa suppressed a sigh of relief. There was suddenly a cacophony of noise from outside of the van.

'What the hell's that?' asked the other man.

'I don't know; I don't like it. I'm going to check it, okay?'

'I think I'll come with you?' said the other man.

'Fine, but shut the doors.'

The two men walked to the back of the van. Clarissa stood up once the door had been closed. She was hoping it was just closed over and she could jump out, maybe catching one man unawares and run off. If she was lucky, they wouldn't even be there. They'd be off investigating whatever distraction Pats had set up. Maybe he could keep it going. She couldn't guarantee that, though.

Clarissa came out from behind the box and walked down the interior of the wagon. She had the light on from the mobile phone because otherwise she wasn't able to see. But when she reached the door, she swore under her breath. They'd closed it properly. She couldn't open it from inside. Quickly, she made her way back behind the box. It was five minutes later when the men came back inside.

'Come on, we need to shift it. You know we've got the ten-minute limit.'

Suddenly, the two smaller boxes beside her were lifted and taken. This was it. Clarissa couldn't wait until they lifted one up and she came out from behind her box, walking down behind the men. The one at the front was only carrying a small box and jumped down straight to the ground, walking off. The man behind him put his down, however. He placed his hands on the interior of the van before swinging his legs out to land on the ground.

Clarissa skulked in the shadows at the side of the van, hoping he wouldn't see her. When he quickly turned to walk away with his box, she was delighted and strode forward, seeing the man disappear round the other side of the van. She jumped down, wincing as her knees felt the drop of a couple of feet.

She went to run, to take a left out of the back of the van when the men had taken a right. However, after two steps, something behind her grabbed, and she nearly went off her feet. Her shawl had caught. A little catch where the door closed into. She turned, pulling at it. It gripped.

She'd have to yank it. It would rip the tartan, but it had to be done. They'd be back any second. She pulled and then pulled again, but it wouldn't come away. Could she unravel herself? *There wasn't time*, she thought. So, she grabbed it again. She pulled, and it ripped, and Clarissa stumbled forward.

She took a tumble, rolling across the gravel path, unaware of quite where she was. It was raining all the time and as she stood up, her shawl was covered, damp and somewhat sticky from the road's surface.

'Who the hell are you?' said a voice suddenly. Clarissa turned, nightstick in hand, pulled back out from underneath her shawl. She swung with it and the man jumped backwards. He then leapt forward, trying to throw a fist at her. But she whirled the nightstick back, catching him on the wrist. He yelled.

She went to turn and run away, but right behind her was the

other man. He had bent down and driven a shoulder straight into her stomach, grabbed her feet and lifted her clean off the ground.

'Boss will not like this,' he said. Clarissa's nightstick dropped, the wind driven out of her. She gasped for breath. The man promptly dumped her inside the van, her head coming down hard on the wooden interior. He pushed her legs in and the door was closed quickly.

'Go!' said a voice from outside. Clarissa tried to get herself up, but the air was knocked out of her. She could feel the wagon beginning to bounce. As it made its way along the road, she was trapped. Where would they take her? The confidence she'd felt earlier on was ebbing away. She'd find out what MacPhail was really like then. She remembered people from back in the day, some of the right, utter bastards. And she'd been on the streets. Well, she'd dealt with them. Albeit, she'd been a heck of a lot younger.

* * *

Patterson looked out of the car window. 'Do we get the lights on?' said Sabine.

'No,' said Patterson. 'We need to follow. They won't stop. They'll drive off and might even finish the poor girl. We tail them since they don't know we're on to them.'

'I'm calling Emmett,' said Sabine. 'Get going.'

'What's Emmett going to do?'

'He can be there. He can bring another vehicle.'

'I don't know what else, because we don't know where we're going.'

'Don't call in uniform. If they get wind, they might just

despatch her. You know what Macleod said about MacPhail?'

'Oh, I know,' said Sabine. Her face was worried and she was right. She rang the number to contact Emmett. Clarissa was a tough nut. But then again, so was this MacPhail character. If the two collided, it wouldn't be good.was never good.

Chapter 20

Clarissa was blindfolded. She knew this because they tied the bind so tight it was cutting into her head. Her head was screaming anyway from having been thumped down on the wooden floor of the van. After that, she had rolled from side to side as the vehicle raced away through the night. It had bounded down a road that had not been smooth, and each pothole was felt on that wooden floor as she bounced about.

When she had come to, after the van had stopped and the doors had been opened, someone had grabbed her quickly and put the blindfold on her. Her hands had been taken behind her back, and with an arm put under each of her armpits, she'd been half carried, half dragged.

She thought it was a stone floor, from the feeling that came across her shoes, and from how cold and hard it was as she was dumped forward. The blindfold was whipped off, but her hands were not unbound, and she was left on the floor. She'd heard a gasp as she'd landed hard, but had thought little about it because her head was ringing.

She was in a dark room, and something was moving beside what seemed to be a metal door. Clarissa rolled onto her back, eyes trying to adjust to the dark. And then a face was over the top of her. Although it was dark, there was enough light to just about see, but she wasn't sure about the face in front of her. It was angelic, a young woman, and she thought she knew it. Was she hallucinating? Was she suddenly seeing the sculpture alive before her eyes? And then this face smiled, but it was a smile etched with concern.

'Are you okay?'

'Do I look okay?' said Clarissa.

'I can't believe they've done that to an old woman.'

'Less of the old. I take it you're Cara.'

'How do you know who I am? Of course. You're that woman. You and that other man were at the flat.'

'Yes. You've stirred up quite a hornet's nest, haven't you?' said Clarissa.

There were tears now in the eyes of the woman, and she turned away from Clarissa.

'I know it's probably not a great time, but you couldn't help me up a bit, could you?' asked Clarissa.

'Maybe you should help her across to the wall, so she could sit up like I can.'

Clarissa recognised the voice. It was the priest. He was here too. And then it dawned on her.

'You were hiding her, weren't you? She was there all the time. That's not good, Father. You shouldn't lie, especially to a police officer.'

'You're with the police?' said Cara.

'Detective Inspector Clarissa Urquhart, currently not in the best of situations. I'm hoping that someone might come for me.'

'We've been here a day,' said Father Kershaw. 'Cara, help her

173

over.

Cara reached down, tears still in her eyes and half-carried, half-dragged Clarissa over to the nearest wall. It was damp and as Clarissa leaned her head back on it, she could feel the moisture through her hair. She breathed in. The smell was pretty rank. She could also smell the urine.

'Sorry,' said the priest. 'They haven't really given us anything. We had to make do with a corner.'

Clarissa simply nodded. 'Why have they let you walk about?' she asked Cara.

'Oh, she's not to be touched,' replied the priest.

'Why?' asked Clarissa.

'I don't know why I've been targeted,' said Cara. 'I just know it's to do with Ernesto. He's the sculptor, and I model for him.'

'I'm well aware of what you do, and it's definitely to do with Ernesto, and I don't know why. Although I've a good idea.'

'I haven't seen him that often recently. He's been busy taking on a lot of work. He gets very involved in his work. A genius, he really is. He went to Kylesku to work on his own sculptures. But he's making other figurines, isn't he? He had other ones up on the shelves. Different ones. He didn't only ever sculpt me. He did sculpt other things. Some animals and things. But they were very his style. But he's done other ones.'

'Yes, he has been doing a lot of those. I've come from . . . spending time with them last night,' said Clarissa.

'He told me he had lots of commissions to do. That's why he couldn't find the time to sculpt me. It was not like him. He'd always find time in the past. We'd always enjoyed those sessions.'

'Why the name?' asked Clarissa. 'Why See'am Moon? Why not Cara? We could have found you quickly. We could have—'

'Because I wanted to get away from it. He said it was best to break away from my old life. I was starting a new one. He was paying me, and I was quite happy. I was able to go to church up in Aberdeen and get on with my own life, out of the way of everything. I wanted a break from the past,' said Cara. 'Ernesto gave me that. Father Kershaw helped me too, but I needed to move on. And then those men came round.'

'Was that the first time you'd met them?'

'Yes.' Clarissa gently smacked her head off the wall, and then thought better of it as the pain rang through her head again.

'Damn it,' she said, 'I think they followed us. They couldn't find you, so they used me. So sorry.

'Ernesto was in trouble. He mentioned something about it. He never said much to me, but he had said he had quit doing these other commissions. Ernesto wanted to go back and do the ones he enjoyed again.'

'What's happening, said Clarissa, 'is that he's been doing sculptures for a man called MacPhail. He's a very nasty piece of work. It's his men that have us in here, Father. I have to tell you, it's not a place we want to be.'

The priest looked over almost knowingly, but Cara seemed a bit bemused. 'I suspect you're not tied up and able to move because they're going to want Ernesto to go back to doing what he did for them before. They can't take away his great love, because he won't do anything then. But they're going to tell him they have you. You'll be okay, Cara, at least for the meantime. I'm not so sure about us, Father. They want rid of me quick. And they won't do it publicly. Put me somewhere where it's hard to find. They'll be awaiting MacPhail's order. You might go with that as well.'

Cara cried. And she ran over to Father Kershaw. The man

couldn't embrace her. Instead, Cara leaned on his shoulder, weeping.

'There's time enough for that when we're gone,' said Clarissa. 'In the meantime, maybe we can work out how to get out of here. Help me up on my feet,' she said to Cara.

Cara came over, sniffing, and hauled Clarissa up. Clarissa's knees were in agony. In fact, her whole body felt battered. What was she doing this for at this time of life? Macleod hadn't even come down either. She was in trouble, real trouble now. She knew it, but retreating, getting scared, wouldn't help the situation. Clarissa felt the binds behind her.

'Cara, can you pull this apart?' Cara reached down, tugging at it.

'It's that plastic stuff. It's like a tie,' she said. 'I can't move it. Not at all. It's really thick.'

'Feels thick,' thought Clarissa. 'It's cutting into my wrists as well. We could go for the old trick when he opens the door.'

'We could,' said Father Kershaw, 'except they push the door open, and they stand outside and wait. Often, they've got a gun. They eye up where you are before they come in.'

'Damn it,' said Clarissa. 'Cara, try underneath my shawl here. Is there a night stick?'

'A what?' she said.

'It's a metal pole. It flicks out into a stick.'

Clara reached up under the shawl. There was nothing. 'There's nothing here at all,' she said.

'Double damn it. Is there a phone?'

'There's nothing under the shawl.'

'Of course they wouldn't leave her phone on her. They couldn't get into it, though, at least not immediately. It was locked out with a code. They'd have to take it to somebody who knew what they were doing.'

'What's going to happen?' asked Cara.

Clarissa thought she'd made that pretty clear. Rather than go over it again. She thought about something different. 'They may take us out, Father. You're going to have to play off my lead. I'm hoping we've been tailed here. If we have, we've got a chance.'

'Well, I hope you brought numbers,' said Father Kershaw, 'because I've seen five different people here.'

Oh, heck, thought Clarissa. 'Even if Pats and Sabine get here, that's a big number. Especially if they have weapons. They might call the team in. Bring a safety. They might want to find out what's going on first.'

Clarissa stopped for a moment and looked around the room. There was a single lightbulb up above her. It was dim and everywhere was dark and slimy. Just where was it here? That would be the difficult bit. As long as they'd tailed her, as long as they'd come, she might be okay.

The metal door swung open. Father Kershaw was right. No one stepped in. Clarissa looked out into the gloom beyond. After ten seconds, a man in a hoodie slowly walked in. A gun in front of him.

'Right, boys. Bring the priest; bring grandma too. Time to go outside. You, the good-looking one, you stay here.'

Clarissa gave Cara a nod, because the girl didn't seem to know what to do. Father Kershaw slowly stepped out in front of Clarissa, and she followed him. *Well,* she thought to herself, *Clarissa, girl, if you're going to do something, you need to do it soon. Because I know what this is. This is execution.*

Chapter 21

Sabine Ferguson was nervous. She donned the black, waterproof jacket and stepped out of the car into the rain. They were approximately five hundred yards from the building the van had gone to. Across from her, Patterson was in a rain jacket too and his hair was dripping wet.

'Did we get back up?'

'We need to find out how she's being held first. I'll tell Emmett we're moving in. He has the coordinates, he'll get here. I can tell him to organise a squad if we need to. We don't want to alert people yet. If we get spotted on the way in, they could just act. They could just kill her.'

'Okay. You're the sergeant,' said Patterson, 'but I don't like this. It's typical of her. I told her to get out. I told her to—'

'Leave it,' said Sabine. 'Doesn't matter now. All that matters is we get there.'

'Have you got your nightstick with you?'

'I have one in my back pocket, but I rarely use them. I fight better with my fists,' said Sabine. 'It's what I do.'

'Well,' said Patterson, 'as someone who's had his throat cut before, I bring every weapon I can nowadays.'

Sabine and Patterson walked through the sodden grass in front of them. There was a small, wooded forest beyond before the house. It looked derelict but there was a car and a van parked outside. The van was the one that had been used to transport the antiques about.

Sabine thought they had done a good job of tailing it at a distance. Being that late at night, it hadn't been easy and when they'd thought for a moment they'd lost it, they'd spotted headlights heading down to this house. A short recce had confirmed the van was there.

They'd made plans to infiltrate and woken Emmett up. He was on his way, but he'd be a couple of minutes out yet and they couldn't wait. Now, as they made their way through the trees, their movements covered by the sound of the pouring rain, Sabine felt she was sweating more inside her jacket than getting rained on the outside.

Sabine, approaching close to the house, stopped just inside the line of the trees. She could see several flashlights behind the house. Some people were being led out, or at least pushed out in front. Sabine peered through the darkness and then saw the outline of a white collar around a man's neck. He was dressed in black, otherwise.

'That's Father Kershaw. What's he doing here? And that's Clarissa behind him. Recognise that shawl anywhere.'

'What about behind them?' whispered Patterson. They peered and saw several figures moving their way forward, forcing Clarissa onto a grassy mound beside the gravel drive-way. It was an open area, but still sheltered away from the road and any prying eyes.

The grassy area they were taking them to was quite a distance from the trees. It would be awkward to get there. Sabine wondered what to do, especially seeing the gun that was raised by the man walking behind. There was him and another three men as well. They were probably armed, too. She couldn't cover this distance in the open.

Clarissa and Father Kershaw were instructed to go towards the grassy mound and were soon on their knees. Their hands were tied up behind them, but the priest was leaning forward, whispering away about something.

'What's he doing?' asked Patterson.

'Oh, hell. That looks like last rites,' said Sabine. 'He's giving the last rites. Patterson, we need to do something. We need to do something quick.'

'What though? What are we going to do? How do we get there? He's got a gun. We'd be dead by the time we reached them.'

'They're going to be dead by the time we get there.' Sabine stood up from her haunches, ready to run forward.

'So what? We just make a suicide run.'

'We make a distraction. Something or other. Patterson, he's lifting the gun. Look!'

The man who had led the party out was now lifting his handgun and stepping over behind Clarissa. It looked for all intents and purposes that he was going to step behind her and despatch her with a shot to the back of the head.

'So what do we do?' asked Patterson.

But he was too late. Sabine was already out of the trees and running, and she was issuing a war cry.

Sabine didn't know if it would work. All she knew was she had to cause a distraction. She had to stop the man from taking the shot. But as she yelled, she saw the other men turning for their guns and running towards her. The first man was continuing towards Clarissa but Sabine was committed. There was no choice now. And she yelled for all she was worth, running towards the armed group.

* * *

What was going on? They hadn't been where he'd expected them to be. Emmett had found the car, but Sabine and Patterson had left. After a short walk, he thought he could see them in the woods, but they were standing off from a clearing.

Emmett decided to scout round the other side of the house. Maybe he could find something over there, or warn them if he saw something untoward. He'd text them. After all, a double vantage position would be better.

He also didn't want to get involved in any fisticuffs, for he wasn't a fighter. Never really good at that sort of thing. When he'd gone through his training, the physical side wasn't something he enjoyed. He'd had to do it, had to come up to scratch. And he could probably throw a punch, or maybe take somebody's arm and drive it up behind their back if he had to.

He was far from the best of them and when he worked with uniform, if they were looking for boys to go out and pick someone up and expecting a scuffle, Emmett generally drove the van or else didn't go at all. He knew he wasn't the strongest. Far from it. And that awareness was something that was healthy. Something that kept his jaw in line from getting hit too often.

The far side of the driveway from where Sabine and Ferguson stood was boggy. Yet the heavy rain meant that the squelching sound Emmett's shoes made as he crept through the grass got eaten up. Probably, no one would hear it. He wasn't using a torch, which made it difficult with foot placement.

As he got closer to the house, he saw the van. They said that Clarissa had got into a van when they briefed him, and she'd been trapped in it. So, Emmett made his way quietly to the rear. There was a bit of a squeak as he opened the rear door, but on looking inside, no one was there. He went round to the front and clambered into the cab. Maybe he'd find something inside that could help.

As he did so, he heard voices. He hunkered down low in the seat as best he could, and looking out of the window, he saw a priest being walked over towards a grassy mound in front of the house.

Then he saw the tartan shawl that followed. Clarissa's hair was soaking wet. Lilac didn't stand out in the darkness and her hair had gone flat, such was the driving rain. Emmett stayed low, and as he did so, he heard a sound as something jiggled. He looked to his left.

They had left the keys in the ignition. That was handy. He watched from the window, as Clarissa and Father Kershaw had to go onto their knees. The man behind was waving his gun about. Someone had a phone out. As he thought about retreating into the darkness, out of the cab, Emmett saw a screaming Sabine Ferguson, charging from the trees on the far side. She was a fair distance away, but approaching quickly. The man at the front of the party was waving his gun, and was making a direct track towards Clarissa.

Emmett's heart thumped, he couldn't jump out, he was unarmed. What could he do? And then he remembered the jiggle. He reached down, turned the ignition of the van and heard the engine roar into life. The van was a seven-and-a-half-ton truck, something Emmett had driven twice. At the gaming conventions he went to, sometimes they needed help. And he'd got the license for it.

He didn't switch on any lights instead, spinning the wheel quickly. Working the clutch and the accelerator, he drove through the first gear onto the second and got the van moving. He clipped the car parked beside it as he moved past, but Emmett didn't care. It was now in second gear and it was speeding up quickly.

Thankfully, the van was empty, so the engine had little to work against. The car was scraped as the side of the van ran up it, but the wheels, grabbing on the gravel track, drove it onward.

The man who was marching towards Clarissa didn't seem to notice. More concerned by the wailing Sabine, he should have noticed, and it would have been a life-saving moment, because Emmett drove the van straight at him. At the last second, the man noticed and turned with his gun pointed towards the windscreen. Emmett ducked. A shot went off, but Emmett heard a body clattered by the van when he looked up again.

His windscreen was intact, and he spun the wheel, placing the van between Sabine and the other men, who were firing their weapons. He ducked again. His windscreen blew out, but he was sure he was somewhere near the men. He heard a clatter; he heard a yell, people screaming. But Emmett just kept the wheel turned tight and his foot on the accelerator.

The van spun round here and there. Emmett didn't know what he was doing, but whatever he was doing was having an effect. There were some more gunshots, then there was a cry of 'get out.' Emmett stayed down low in the van.

* * *

Sabine Ferguson couldn't believe her eyes. She started crying but rolled for cover when the shots were fired. The first man had been hit by the van. The next few seconds were a bit of a blur as the van spun round. It hit another two of the men and then there were shouts to get away, cries of panic.

Sabine got back up to her feet, using the van as a form of shield. There were still some shots, and she stayed low, hoping that Patterson hadn't joined her. She didn't look back, watching those ahead of her in case they were shooting in her direction.

Soon everything was quiet, except for some yells, cries of retreat, moans of pain. The man who had his gun pointed at Clarissa was gone. Sabine saw him limping off into the distance. Clarissa had got up after hearing the impact of the van on him, shouted at Father Kershaw, and the two of them had run off into the wood. Hopefully, Patterson would have gone towards them.

As Sabine arrived at the van, she looked at the front; the window blown out, glass was everywhere. She opened the door at the side, using it first as a shield in case anyone was looking towards her. Then she glanced round. In the driver's well, bowled up tight, was Emmett.

'This way, you need to come this way,' said Sabine. Emmett moved slowly, too slowly for Sabine. He tried to clamber out and eventually she reached, grabbed him by his jacket, pulling him out.

She heard a shout from the woods. It was Patterson. 'I've got Clarissa. I've got the priest,' he said.

'Cara is inside,' yelled Clarissa. 'We need to get inside. Round the back where I came from. Go, Sabine, go.'

Sabine indicated Emmett should follow her and, despite his

rather unenthusiastic eyes, she heard him keep up as she ran over towards the building. At each corner, she would jerk her head round and then would engage in a full sprint to the next one.

As soon as she was inside, the dampness of the building and the fusty sting on the eyes impacted her nostrils as soon as she entered. She kept her focus, eyes wide, pushing through each room. Most had wooden doors that had half rotted through. There were sofas that looked destroyed. The place was basically abandoned, until she saw one room with a metal door. It wasn't locked as she pulled it open but she stood clear in case someone was inside.

When she peered through, she saw a dark room with one light on. There was no one there. No one. Quickly, she went through the rest of the house. They were gone. That would have been the cell or prison room. A metal door that didn't fit the rest of the house. When she got back out to the front, Clarissa looked at her. 'Cara? Where's Cara?'

'Nobody inside,' said Sabine. 'No one.'

'Then they've got her,' said the priest from behind Clarissa. 'What will they do with her?'

'Nothing,' said Clarissa. 'They were treating her with kid gloves. You and me, they would have killed. You and me. Not her. They need her. They're wanting Ernesto to sculpt for them. To create counterfeits. Copies. Really good ones. use her. She'll be okay. At least until Ernesto does something stupid like refuse or escapes himself.'

'Do you think they have him?' asked Patterson.

'They've been following us and reaching out. They'll have him,' said Patterson. 'I'm sure of it. That's why they went for her. Why would you want her unless you'd got him and he refused. She's his muse. He would guarantee her safety.'

'So what do we do?'

'We go for MacPhail. We take what we've got and we go for MacPhail. We get a raid. Come on,' she said.

'Excuse me,' said Patterson.

'What,' said Clarissa.

'You were damn reckless. I told you to get out of there. I told you.'

'It would have been fine, but my shawl caught,' said Clarissa. 'Don't have time for this, Pats. Come on.'

Patterson reached and grabbed her shoulder spinning her back round. 'You were almost dead. Dead except for me and Sabine following you.'

'And you would have been dead except I held my hand on your throat for however long. It's not like I owe you one,' said Clarissa. 'This job, it gets bad, it gets . . .'

'If I can just interject,' said Emmett.

'What?' said Clarissa, testily.

'Maybe the time to do this would be afterwards. When people are less hot-headed. When people are ready to talk about things and come to a more reasonable conclusion.'

Clarissa looked at him, shaking her head. 'You don't like how I roll? Don't bother coming.' She turned and stormed off.

Patterson shook his head. 'Damn woman,' he said, as he took the priest by the arm, leading him back to their car.

Sabine picked up her phone. 'Don't try something like that. Clarissa's Clarissa. You're going to have to accept the way she is. Better get Uniform here, though, and sort this out. She'll want me to do it.'

'You've been up for a while. I've had a sleep,' said Emmett. 'I'll call them in and I'll check what's going on. I'd better make sure that the raid's organised properly. I'm not sure those two are in the best of frame of mind.'

'No, and I'm not either,' said Sabine. She put her hand up. 'Thank you.'

'That's really hers to say.'

'Well, I'm thanking you for that but you probably saved mine too. You pulled cover. You pulled them away from me when I was trying to do a battle cry to save her.'

'Of course,' said Emmett. 'I'm sure you'd have done the same for me.'

Sabine didn't know why, but she suddenly felt like embracing him. She hugged Emmett, who didn't really know what to do. Then she stepped back from him. She smiled at him.

'You did good. Really good. Let's get some support.'

As she walked away, she looked back at Emmett. He was already making his way over to the van, ready to look at the detail of what had happened. The man had saved her life, he'd saved Clarissa's, and yet it looked like he'd just come back from the shopping. Sabine smiled.

He was under her skin, not that she wanted to pursue anything with him, but she found herself unable to not like him. If he'd made a move towards her, if he indicated any sort of feeling towards her, she thought she might actually fall for him. But that wasn't him. He was just a genuinely decent guy. But he didn't seem to want anything from her. She smiled. He was a rare one in this world. Definitely a rare one.

Chapter 22

I t had taken the rest of the night and some of the morning for Clarissa to organise all the paperwork and clearances to begin a search on MacPhail's properties. She'd had to report what she'd been doing, where she'd been, and what action had been taken on her. But by eleven o'clock that morning, they were all ready to go.

They would attack several of his places, Clarissa taking the lead by raiding MacPhail's rather palatial house on the edge of Glasgow. She was looking forward to this, although she'd calmed down somewhat from earlier on. She had decided this would be her retribution, to take down the man who had basically ordered her death. Of course, she couldn't prove that bit of it, but she believed Ernesto was being kept by him.

The rest of the team were at other locations belonging to MacPhail. Clarissa had consulted at the Glasgow station with those who were used to his methods about where he would hold people. But she wanted to get into his house.

She had a feeling that this was a little more personal than usual. After all, Janice Stewart was not simply a partner in crime. It appeared he was bedding her as well. Everything just felt different from how they described MacPhail. Ernesto still being alive, not simply rejected as far as she could tell. And then Cara, not being tied up, being treated well. But then again, if MacPhail could run this racket, he would earn an absolute fortune off Ernesto, illegally, immorally. But then again, MacPhail was about the money.

The house was spectacular. One of those that probably had six or seven bathrooms, although Clarissa didn't count them. There were certainly more rooms here than the man needed. There was also, when they raided, several women upstairs. They were pretty shocked, but then again, they were maybe glad to be leaving.

There was also a rather tall blonde in her forties, and a few children as well. Clarissa was reliably informed that this was MacPhail's family, whereas Janice Stewart was his fancy bit on the side. Clarissa didn't move into these worlds very often. Hers was usually a world where people were doting on the art, not simply using it.

Even last time, with the jewel called the Esoteric Tear, the case had been full of people who loved the art. They had placed such an importance on it they actually thought it was a cosmic jewel. She guessed they were nuts in a different way.

What was it about artwork that could cause people to go this way? Either treat it as a mere thing to earn them cash, or to think it was everything, not simply a joyous work to be enjoyed. *Money corrupted everything*, thought Clarissa.

When she entered the reception hall of the house, MacPhail actually greeted her. The man was taller than she suspected, reaching six feet two. He had grey hair that was immaculately kept, and he was wearing a suit that spoke of money.

The reception hall was decadent but not classy. It had a marble staircase and had various of what were probably assumed to be cultured items around. To Clarissa, they were expensive knick-knacks. And on one side there was a large Trojan horse. It had been in Janice Stewart's studio and now here it was in the hallway. It was a hideous thing. No class about it at all.

'I see you're not an art collector,' said Clarissa.

The man glared at her. 'It's funny, I heard you were down this way. I didn't think you'd bring so many friends with you, though.'

'People like you, you don't deserve art. You don't deserve any of this. Well actually, you can keep all of it. What is that thing?' she said, pointing to the Trojan horse.

'Some of us just like art in a big way. Some of us know what to keep hold of. We can see the prize inside.'

'I don't think so. I don't think you can see anything except pound signs, but we'll find him.'

'Who?'

'Ernesto Hunter,' said Clarissa. 'Oh, you're well aware of his work.'

MacPhail's wife walked up beside him, putting her hand on his shoulder. 'Everything all right, darling?'

'Everything's fine. Our Scottish friend here just seems to get carried away with herself.'

'I'm totally carried away with myself,' said Clarissa. 'Here. Some of your warehouses. Oh yes, Janice Stewart's. Searching her studio and her private areas, and her private dwelling as well. Hope we don't find anything of yours there.'

'I'm sure you won't,' said MacPhail. 'I've never been there.'

'Don't worry, love,' said Clarissa to MacPhail's wife, 'if he's left anything behind, I'll drop it back to you first.'

Clarissa could see the thunder in MacPhail's face. Was it an open secret, or did he keep everything of that ilk on the quiet? His wife looked a little shocked. *Could you be living with a man like this, and still be shocked at what he did.*

It took most of the day, but at five o'clock MacPhail stood beside Clarissa once again. 'Not find anything, then. Anywhere? Harder to find a second time. Harder to come back.'

'You've got him somewhere. I know you've got him and you've got her. You lay a finger on them . . .'

'And you'll what? Parade your shawl through here again. You're not even at home. Take yourself back up to the Highlands.'

'I'm more at home than you know,' said Clarissa, unsure what that even meant. She didn't normally trade blows though the one to his wife earlier on in the day had been a good one. The only annoying thing was nobody had found any of MacPhail's at Janice Stewart's. Otherwise, she would have brought it over in a plastic bag. But ultimately, at the end of it all, she needed to find Ernesto.

What would MacPhail do now? Would he cut and run? Clarissa walked out of the house down the rather large driveway, standing somewhere near the bottom. She took out her phone, calling the Inverness station. According to his secretary, Macleod was busy. But she kept on saying she needed him now. It was twenty minutes, and he eventually rang back.

'Am I the B team now?' asked Clarissa.

'I'm packing, and busy. I need to go, okay? Things have kicked off here on something.'

'Kicked off on what? The others weren't doing anything. I didn't think Hope had anything on the go.'

'I can't talk about it, all right? It's just something else I do. What?'

'I told you we were doing the raid. It's come up with nothing.'

'Well, that's a surprise,' said Macleod.

'But he's got them. He's got them somewhere.'

'Well, re-look at it then. Go back over everything. Find them. Find them. Wherever he's holding them.'

'But we've been everywhere.'

'Clarissa, have you talked to Glasgow? Have you talked to the guys at that station? Don't go to the obvious. Go to everywhere else as well. Go to everywhere.'

'Sure, I've done this sort of thing before. You know? I have talked to these people.'

'Well, what are you wanting from me then?'

'A bit of support.'

'Well, this is it. This is your phone call.'

'I don't want a phone call. I want you down here, sat here talking to me. I want you with me. People jump when you're there.'

'I've got an Italian case on the go. I need to deal with it. Jane hasn't even got my attention at the moment. You're lucky I'm picking up this call.'

'Seoras, don't do that to me. I'm calling you in. You owe me. You owe me for that stunt with your head.'

Clarissa was referring to a previous case where Macleod had faked his own death with a false head and an apparent beheading. She hadn't forgiven him for it and she'd damn well make him pay for it.

'I don't care,' said Macleod. 'This one I've got to go to.'

'Look, are you blowing me off?'

'Okay, I hear you,' said Macleod, 'but I can't come down. And besides, I don't even know the situation.'

'You realise this is MacPhail? This is like the guy half of

Glasgow station is after. To shut this guy down—even though it would be on half of nothing to do with what he actually does—it would be a heck of a coup. You'd have your name on it.'

Clarissa smacked her head with her palm. *Don't do that to Seoras*, she thought.

'Are you talking fame? Are you seriously trying to dangle fame in front of me?' said Macleod. 'You know me better than that. If I say I've got to go, I've got to go. I don't mess about. I realise it's MacPhail. And I want you to get him. But you need to go back and pull everything together. You've got it this far. And I understand why. He's got someone. But he's not stupid. He'll be there.'

'Did you ever tangle with him?' asked Clarissa. 'Have you got any insight?'

Macleod went quiet for a moment. And then he said, 'Go with him. Whatever you do, be aware that he will try to show he's cleverer than you. He will try to put what he's done in front of you. He can't help it. Then he'll do it because he thinks it's so good at it.

'I got him once. Just once. It was something very minor and they got away with it in court. Pulled up for some discrepancy and some poor officer hadn't followed the rules correctly. You need to understand that he will be wanting to wave it in your face without you recognising it. He gets off on that. Has he got a mistress at the moment?'

'Yes, he has. I dropped it in front of his wife.'

Macleod laughed. 'He won't like that. He really won't like that. But that's good. Because he'll keep coming back at you. He will want to demean you. Especially someone like you.'

'Why someone like me?' said Clarissa.

'He's a city boy. Classy suits. You? You look like . . . the posh people from the country.'

'No I do not!'

'Tartan shawl, tartan trews. Purple hair. Drives an impressive car. Oh, you're money from the country to him. The sort that don't like him. Keep him down. He'll want to rub this in your face, completely. Let him. Let him bring it on. He'll drop the ball and you need to be ready. Be clever on this one. But make sure, make sure, when you reveal it, he can't get out of it.'

'Okay,' said Clarissa, ' but as soon as you're done in Italy, get your backside down here.'

'I think you're mistaking me for a DI again. I'm the DCI. The "C" in the middle is very important,' said Macleod. 'And I'm off to Italy. I'm on the phone. But, please, only if necessary. I need my head together on this one.'

Clarissa wondered what he was doing, but she knew better than to ask. He'd have said exactly otherwise.

'Fair enough. I've got the new boy with me, anyway. See if I can put him to good use.'

'Emmett?' said Macleod. 'I passed him by once. Never quite got him. Let me know how he gets on.'

'Well, he's with us now.'

'He took the job because we had to put him somewhere. He doesn't really fit in. I don't know if he'll fit in with you either,' said Macleod. 'When I get back, you can tell me what you think of him?'

Clarissa refrained from saying he'd saved her life that day already. Macleod didn't need to know those things. Not at the moment. Not when she wanted him. When she needed him for something and he wasn't playing ball.

Macleod closed down the call and Clarissa turned and looked back at the house. Screw his driveway. Screw his posh house. He'd been running Glasgow left, right, and centre for however long. He would not do it anymore. She was going to nail him. This posh country woman was going to take down the city boy. She was glad she'd spoken to Macleod. She didn't understand MacPhail. Maybe she was beginning to. Maybe she'd have to call him out. She could search again, but not on this basis. She needed another way. Time to talk to the team.

Chapter 23

'He likes to put it in your face. He says that he'll show it to us. The one thing he'll do is, if he thinks he has it over us, he'll drop clues. He'll make it so obvious, except it's not. He tries to be clever. You can see that with the money,' said Clarissa. 'Macleod said he won't like me, because I'll be like a country toff, all in tartan. He doesn't like somebody from outside the city. He thinks he's above everyone.'

The team was sitting in the small office in the Glasgow station, and Emmett was the first to reply. 'With all due respect, Detective Inspector, I've not known you for that long, but you don't seem that sort of person. You seem a bit more rough and—'

'Rough and what? Ready?' said Clarissa. 'Don't mistake country classy enthusiasm for rough and ready.'

'Of course not,' said Emmett, looking a little bemused. 'But what is it you want to do?'

'Exactly,' said Sabine. 'We've searched everywhere. That was an extensive search. They will not let us go back and do the same sort of search again, not without fresh evidence, and that doesn't seem to be forthcoming.'

'No, it's not. But we need a reason to get back in.' said

196

Clarissa, 'we need something that allows us to go in and to deal with this, and to find what we want to find.'

'Perhaps,' said Patterson, 'you're going about this the wrong way. We made it all about our missing persons. But it's not, is it? It's not all about our missing persons. It's all about the art. We didn't go looking in for the pieces of art. We went looking for two people who disappeared. What if we can get the art together? What if we can turn round and say, look, all this fake art's being produced. Therefore, we need to search again.'

'Yes,' said Clarissa. 'We need to do our first search, searching for art. The fact we might find some people who have gone missing along the way is entirely another matter.'

'And search his house again,' said Emmett.

Clarissa looked at him. 'But we know they're not there. I personally supervised that search.'

'Look,' said Emmett. 'I'm not suggesting you did anything wrong. All I'm suggesting is that we need to go to him. We need you in front of him to get him riled. We need him to tell us more. He's going to want to put it in your face, as you just said. Therefore, look as if you're feeling beaten down.'

'Well, that will not be difficult at the moment, will it?' said Clarissa. 'Practically there.'

'Well, you could say that. But, on the other hand—'

'What?' asked Clarissa.

'Well, on the other hand, what you have to be aware of is that he won't know that. Turn it into a game with him. Pretend you're playing along. Maybe he'll flinch. Maybe he'll give you more,' said Emmett.

'But we still need to know how we're going to get in. We still need to get the pieces,' said Clarissa. 'We still need to show corruption on a massive scale.'

'Let me get into the records,' said Emmett. 'Let me sit and go through them. You go visit him. Just pay a visit to wind him up. I'll stay here, get through the records, cross-reference them, present them so we can get permission to search again. But on the arts front. And you don't go with it,' said Emmett. 'Get Sabine to take it in. Get Sabine to ask for the permission.'

'You're becoming a right delight, Emmett. You know that?' said Clarissa. 'You're a devious little one. Right. You stay here with Sabine. Pats, you're with me. We're going to visit our man again.'

'You sure you don't want Sabine with you?' said Patterson.

'Of course not. I need you. You're my man. My go-to guy. After all, you're the one who can stand there with a straight face. We're like a double team, you and me, Pats. Haven't you worked that out yet?'

'Well, I thought I was your fall guy.'

Clarissa looked at him. 'Don't push your luck,' she said.

The little green sports car raced its way out to the edge of Glasgow again. It was now the middle of the next day, a Sunday, and Clarissa hoped MacPhail was eating lunch. She drove up the large driveway, aware that cameras were already watching her, and as she parked out in front of the front door, a doorman approached.

'Excuse me, madam, the family are not entertaining visitors today. Mr MacPhail is engaged with the family.'

'Tell Mr MacPhail his favourite Scottish landowner is here.'

'I'm afraid, madam—'

Clarissa brushed her way past the man, storming towards the door. She pushed it open, stepping out into the vestibule and almost rearing again against the massive Trojan horse on the side. *Who in their right mind would put that in here?* she

198

thought. She marched on through, opening several doors, until she was approached by a couple of burly men.

'I think you might want the door on the left,' said Patterson. 'I think I can hear the clank of cutlery. They may be having Sunday lunch.'

'Now, gentlemen,' said Clarissa to the two burly men, 'I'm going through that door. Don't stop me.'

She stepped forward, and one of them stepped across her. Clarissa rammed her foot hard down on his toe. He merely grimaced and went to grab her, until he realised he was being prodded with something in the stomach.

'It's a bit like a taser,' she said, 'you'll probably fall on the floor and wet yourself, but you're attacking a woman, and it won't look good for you.'

She opened the door before the man could react any further. MacPhail was sitting at the head of a table with his wife at the other end and several kids were perched in the middle. They were eating what looked like roast beef, and good quality roast beef, from Clarissa's point of view. She heard Patterson walk into the room behind her, but her eyes were only on one person. MacPhail was sitting in a waistcoat and tie.

'To what do I owe this intrusion? Can't a family have their own time on a blessed Sunday?'

'You haven't seen a blessed Sunday in your life. If you did, the chapel would kick you out.'

'I think we can withhold the abuse,' said MacPhail. 'My children are present.'

'Well, apologies to them,' said Clarissa. 'Spending Sunday with the family. It's not where you spend your nights, is it?'

MacPhail stood up at that one. 'Just because you haven't found what you've been looking for. And you won't find it.

You won't find it at all. It's like a myth, isn't it? It's like a story you heard once, you didn't think to be true. But it's not true. They're not here,' he said. 'I don't just wheel people about here, there, wherever.'

'Does this make up for it?' said Clarissa, turning to MacPhail's wife. 'The family moments. You're looking at a woman here and to me, I don't think it cuts the mustard. Unless you're really looking for the money. And if that's the case,' said Clarissa, turning back to MacPhail, 'I guess you've a problem.'

'If you're just here to hurl insults, then get out,' said MacPhail, 'or I'll have you removed. Take you for harassment.'

'Harassment,' said Clarissa. 'Is that what you city boys call it? Can't handle yourselves. Can't take the heat of the competition, can you? It's a shame. Well, I'll tell you now. We're going to find them. I know you have them. Both of them. People won't get so upset about Ernesto, though. After all, he's a great artist, but few of us can fully appreciate great art. You, for instance. But he's also terrific at copying stuff, isn't he? Fortunate for you, you had somebody to tell you that. When did Janice tell you? Before you got into bed with her? Or after?'

Clarissa knew that the two largest burly men from outside were now flanking her and MacPhail was looking to them.

'You're right,' said Clarissa. 'Children here, don't want to make daddy look bad in front of the kids, do I?'

'You haven't got anything, have you?' said MacPhail. 'You have no idea. So you thought you'd come in and just wind me up? Somebody told me you worked for Macleod.'

'And what of it?' asked Clarissa.

'Back in the day, I met him. Do you know what? He was better than you. Yeah, he wasn't as punchy with his jibes, but they cut. Sanctimonious. But you, you're toothless with ears.'

'Enjoy the beef,' said Clarissa. 'I'd get it all used up out of the freezer, though. Where Dad's going, they don't do beef, especially not on a Sunday.'

She turned on her heel, walking past Patterson. He had the look of a rather disturbed man on his face. She knew he wasn't comfortable with this. Patterson was more by the book. He didn't like the cajole. He'd find what he needed, and then he went to ask you. Not this way.

'So,' said Clarissa as they walked out through the vestibule, 'what do we do then? Do we come back again? Or do we hit him with the search next time?'

'When we get back to the office,' said Patterson, 'the heat will be on us. You know he's probably got some people in the force to talk to. You don't get to his sort of level of influence without somebody coming after you. Without someone you can lean on when times get tough. Of course, he's got someone somewhere in the force.'

'Okay, Pats, we've given Emmett a while. Let's see what he comes up with.'

On her return to the office, Clarissa stared at the wall. Emmett had gone through everything. He'd sent Sabine along with several other officers to catalogue. They catalogued everything that was in the arts storerooms, and in the studios and auction houses. Most of them had online catalogues and Emmett had pulled them all in together and drawn them all up on the wall. He had rings around all the ones they suspected to be fake.

'He's been busy. Although I don't think they're all Ernesto's. Maybe he's just one of a group of people. Maybe he's the one who stepped out of line. Because there's too many here for

201

just him to have done them.'

'Maybe he's doing the superb ones,' said Clarissa. 'Well, what do we do now, then? Now we know or suspect that all these are fake.'

'I don't know,' said Emmett. 'I mean, we're going have to get a hold of them. This is your world, not mine.'

Patterson smiled at Sabine who gave a worried look back. 'What are you thinking?' he asked.

'We need evidence to get our new search. Let's get it. Get on the phone to every person in this business of ours who really knows what they're about. Every expert. Line them up with all the targets here and ask them if they're real. Get signed statements detailing them. Tomorrow morning, we head out with them to all of these locations and show them. When they come back and they say these are fake, we take that put that in front of those who can grant us the search and then we get back at him. That's how we get MacPhail.'

Sabine and Clarissa spent the rest of the day on the phone while Emmett and Patterson organised the next day. They realised they'd have to move in everywhere at the same time. Accommodation was booked that night. On the quiet, transport was arranged.

The very next morning from various hotels across Glasgow, experts in their field examined the pieces. The evidence was flooding back within an hour, and Emmett rounded it up and gave it to Clarissa in a nicely presented format. She disappeared off to get her permission to search again. She came back and waved it at everyone. 'Got it.'

'But what's it giving us permission to search for?' asked Emmett.

'Artwork. Counterfeit artwork. We'll hammer him for it.'

'It won't be linked to him, though, will it?' said Sabine.

'I'd be surprised if it was,' said Pats. 'But I think what we need to do is do it, anyway. Ruffle his feathers. And then search while we're there for our two missing people.'

'Pull them all in. Get the uniform ready. We'll go in about an hour and a half.' Sabine and Patterson headed out of the office to arrange the numbers. And Clarissa walked over to Emmett, shaking him by the hand.

'It's superb work. You've got that sort of mind, haven't you?'

'Cataloguing, yeah. I like tables. I enjoy formatting. But I do more than that,' he said.

'Well, one thing I've found about you is that you certainly can pull together a lot of stuff I can't. I'm too chaotic,' said Clarissa.

'Maybe,' said Emmett, 'but I'm giving you the chance to get back in. You're going to have to read him. You're going to have to find out where they are. I don't think we're going to get back a third time.'

' I think you're right,' said Clarissa. She thought about where she should be. Part of the search was to be in MacPhail's house. MacPhail was going to be there, surely. She'd take a risk on it.

'I'll deal with MacPhail, front and centre,' said Clarissa. 'The rest of you can organise the other searches.'

'What are you going to do now?' asked Emmett.

Clarissa sat down in Sabine's seat. She put her feet up on the desk, sat back and closed her eyes.

'I'm going to think where he's got them. I'm going to think of everything he said. Because Macleod said he would rub it in my face. And I'm also going to get dressed up to look as much of a country lady as I can.'

Chapter 24

Clarissa arrived in her little green car, ahead of several police cars. Before she had even reached the steps of the house, she saw MacPhail stepping out through the large double doors, almost awaiting her. As she got out of the car, he called to her.

'This is getting ridiculous,' he said. 'You can't just pop in whenever you want.'

'Oh, the last one, interrupting your lunch wasn't sanctioned. This one is. We're going to have another game of find the ball, wherever you've hidden it.'

'You wouldn't find a ball wherever you were. You wouldn't know the prize was inside.'

Clarissa glowered at him. He was baiting her, and Ernesto was here, definitely here.

'I believe you've got certain counterfeit items on the property. That is what we are searching for'

'I thought you were looking for a man and his muse.'

'You're confusing this with the last search,' said Clarissa. 'This is entirely different. You have various works of art that aren't works of art. That's the thing about you city boys. You wouldn't know art if it came up and hit you between the eyes.

Knowing good art comes naturally to us country girls.'

'Why don't you just get out of the city then, if you know what's good for you. Lots of country girls come to the city, and it doesn't work out for them. They struggle to watch their backs; things happen when they don't expect it. It's not the same; maybe there aren't the niceties, the genteel lifestyle,' said MacPhail. 'The city's hard.'

Clarissa walked up to him, so no one else could hear. 'I know the city's hard, I walked these streets. You, however, are beyond the pale, and that's why I'm here, so don't give me any of your nonsense. She's here, and Ernesto is here, and I will find them.'

Clarissa turned to her team. 'Right, you know what you're looking for? If you find any of these artworks, you show them to me, or to one of the other inspectors we have with us. Those who understand the trade, okay? If you're not sure, identify it and make sure it doesn't go walkabout. I'm sure Mr MacPhail will show us where he keeps all of his delightful art collection.'

'Mr MacPhail is doing nothing for you. You'll have to find this prize on your own. I'm going to open no doors for you. Just so you know, there may be the odd trap.'

He was baiting her, she was sure of it. Clarissa couldn't get in her head exactly what it was but something was bugging her. She went in through the door, and saw that rather gross Trojan horse again. It wasn't a fake, so to speak. There just hadn't been one like that before. She turned to him as MacPhail followed her into the building. 'Who in their right mind would buy that?'

'You seem to have something against my wife.'

'Has she visited Janice's studios?'

'As you can see, they get on well together.'

205

'Oh, really,' said Clarissa. 'She didn't look that way the other night. It's one thing when you play behind a woman's back, but when everybody else knows it and puts it in their face, that's when things come home to roost,'

'Just get it done, and get it done quick,' said MacPhail, clearly beginning to tire of her.

The next hour was spent going through the house. Clarissa found only two items that were not original. When she came back to the vestibule, MacPhail was staring at her.

'One of the things, isn't it,' he said. 'All this subterfuge to find stuff, and all you had to do was take a look through the legs and find the door.'

As she was standing, looking over at the Trojan horse, he was baiting her; it was so obvious. She stepped under the legs of the giant horse, and through to the wall beyond it. Her hands traced round, and then she found the groove of a line,

'Something's not right here,' she said.

Clarissa looked up and saw the little hatch in the underside of the Trojan horse. She pulled the hatch down and found inside a button. It was the second interior body of the horse; she pressed it and a door in the wall, just beyond the horse's legs, opened.

'Really,' she said, 'you're seriously telling me that this was your great plan?' She opened the door.

Inside, she could see a well-lit room. Many sculptures were sitting around on pedestals and shelves. Clarissa walked round, donned her gloves and began to examine them all. It took well over an hour but she was on form. She could easily recognise that more than half of them were fakes. A couple of them, beyond that, were fantastic fakes. And there was the odd one thrown in, which must have been a genuine purchase.

'You like them, do you? You never struck me as an art man,' said Clarissa.

'What can I say? The wife has a passion for collecting items like that.'

Clarissa invited the other art experts in, and they all soon agreed that MacPhail had a collection that said it was worth hundreds of thousands, possibly into the millions. Except it wasn't. It was all fake.

'We'll have to check your records, how you buy and sell, but you'll get done for this.'

'I think you'll find that all the purchases are in my wife's name,' said MacPhail.

'That'll be handy for you, won't it? Get her out of the way so Janice and you can have a bit of time together'

'You almost sound jealous.''

Clarissa, however, was deflated. She hadn't found Ernesto and she hadn't found Cara. She came out and stood in the middle of the vestibule. Walking up behind her, MacPhail whispered in her ear.

'They said they called you Macleod's Rottweiler. You get your teeth into somebody, you don't let go and you shake and shake and shake. Imagine my disappointment. That's what you are—you're a disappointment.'

'The DCI said you weren't worth the time, but he said you would boast and give stuff up, and you have done.'

'None of this matters,' said MacPhail, 'I haven't got him, I'll soon make new stuff, send it elsewhere; after all, it's not my name; it's not me they're coming after.'

He was right, of course, and Clarissa stepped outside. The other members of the art team had returned, confiscating various items that were in MacPhail's other properties.

'So, you found a storeroom,' said Sabine.

'Yes, not that it helps our two missing people. He led me up to it, though, as well. Macleod said he would drop stuff in, but it was too easy. There's a Trojan horse. No legs. I found a button.'

She stopped speaking. 'Are you okay?' Patterson asked.

'No. No, no, no,' said Clarissa. 'The wee rat.'

Clarissa marched in and looked up at the Trojan horse. She walked around to the front of it, followed by MacPhail.

'I thought you didn't like this. Not your sort of thing. Big and tasteless, eh? Catch in your throat, does it, that I have stuff like this? But you have got nothing on me.'

Clarissa looked up at the horse's head. The nostrils weren't filled in. This was marble, stone. It would be filled in. Instead, there seem to be gaps.

'Remarkable and lifelike.' Clarissa turned to MacPhail. 'Don't you think it's great the way they chisel out the nostril, even on the horse, all the way through? It does go all the way through, doesn't it? I mean, that's what proper sculptors do.'

'It's a fantastic piece,' said MacPhail.

'I think it's phenomenal,' said Clarissa. 'Very clever.'

'What do you mean?' asked MacPhail.

'The dummy switch. That's genius. Macleod said you'd dangle it in front of my face. And I thought you had done. And that's why I left the room. You almost had me wondering if we'd got the right people. I have to understand what you're doing. You thought if you gave me all the artworks that I would go. Or maybe you'd been advised that I couldn't search again. Would you move them at that point? You've kept them here, haven't you? You've kept them here because things got too hot.'

'What are you talking about?' said MacPhail.

Clarissa traced the Trojan horse round the underside of the belly at the switch. Then she worked her hands towards its rear. Soon she found a line that was incredibly thin.

'What do we have now? Look at it. It's fantastic. Around the back here, we actually have a hole. You can pass air through this. You can maybe even pass other things.'

She turned, walked over to Patterson. 'Go to my car, open up the boot, get me my hammer.'

'What are you going to do?' said Patterson.

'Pats, you're going to see proper detective work. Get me that hammer.'

Patterson shook his head. Clarissa felt he was doing this all the time.

'Thank you.' When he came back ten minutes later with a hammer, Clarissa turned, looked at MacPhail and raised her hand with the hammer in it.

'You can't do that on me. Put that hammer down!'

Clarissa ignored him, turned and threw the hammer into the side of the Trojan horse. There was a loud crack followed by a clang as the hammer hit the floor. Clarissa walked over, picked it up again, and started smacking it against the side of the Trojan horse. There were cracks along the artwork and eventually a piece in the side fell out. Clarissa bent down slightly to shout into the hole.

'It's fine. It's me, DI Clarissa Urquhart. Time for you to come home. I'm sure you've loved it in there.'

Slowly, the face of Ernesto Hunter, appeared. It was followed by Cara's face.

'Well then, Mr MacPhail. Isn't that a coincidence? And a first, I think. Seems to me you've been harbouring, or rather kidnapping and hanging on to, certain people we want to talk to. You're going to have difficulty explaining this one, and inside your own house. You played too many things close to your chest, but the prize was inside, thank you.' Clarissa turned to Patterson. 'Take Mr MacPhail for questioning,' she said.

'Sabine, sort out his guests from within the horse. I'm off to tell his wife.'

Clarissa laughed heartily, and then she turned and stood looking back at MacPhail. She flung her tartan shawl around her again. 'Country girls, they always come out on top.'

Chapter 25

'I can't speak for long. Besides, it'll cost a fortune. I'm in Italy.'

'We've wrapped it up,' said Clarissa. I think the area commander down here in Glasgow is ready to give me keys to the city. MacPhail's going to do time for this one.'

'Well done,' said Macleod. 'Well done.'

'Just well done. I'm going to get breakfast for this one,' said Clarissa.

'Breakfast will be on me, but I'm too busy. I'm not flying back from Italy. Grab a takeaway on your way back up the road.'

Clarissa laughed. 'Oh no, Seoras. We're dining out on this one. This'll be a feather in your cap.'

'If I've still got a cap when I get back,' he said. 'Anyway, well done to you. Wrap it all up, send me the report. And then when you get back up to Inverness, check up on Hope, make sure they're okay.'

'Why? What are they doing?' asked Clarissa.

'Not enough. Hasn't been a murderer up there in at least a week.'

'You're being funny. But as usual, the humour isn't up to

much.'

'Seriously though, where were they? Where was he keeping them?' asked Macleod.

'Inside a Trojan horse. I think he whipped them in there at the first sign of us coming for him. They weren't in there permanently. He was treating Cara well. Trying to keep Ernesto sweet. The trouble with kidnapping the artistic types is some of them see death as quite an interesting work of art. The way in which you die, the legacy you leave behind. MacPhail didn't get that as much as he should have because he wasn't an artist.'

'You saved a relatively young man and you also saved a young girl. And you stopped the passing out of some rather dodgy artworks from what I can gather.'

'I've saved them all up and I'll be sending them up to you for your house, seeing as you wouldn't know them from Adam.'

'Got to go,' said Macleod. 'Bye. Clarissa, well done. That's why I made you DI. You were always more than DS material.'

Clarissa closed down the call, gave herself a smile, and then told herself off for it. He'd done that again, hadn't he? She was angry with him. Angry when he'd apparently lost his head. Angry then that he wouldn't come down to help her out. And then she was smiling, taking praise from him. He could do that, Macleod. He could play you. Work you well.

Not that it was a bad thing. You were doing a job. But he was making sure it got done. She looked up at her team sitting in the small office. There was a bottle of champagne on the desk and the local police chief had come down from the top office briefly to say thank you.

Sabine handed Clarissa a glass of champagne. 'Very kind of you,' she said. 'Many bosses wouldn't do this.'

'Don't thank me,' she said. 'Thank DCI Macleod. Very generous man.'

Patterson nearly spat out his drink. 'Macleod bought this? But he doesn't even go for alcohol.'

'Well, he's not here, and I thought I would take the chance to think what he would do for the team. So I bought it. The bill's on the way to him. I'm sure he'll find it in his heart to cover the expense.'

Sabine smiled but she noticed that Emmett wasn't drinking much. 'Are you sure you don't want some?' she said.

'No,' said Emmett.

'Why not?' asked Sabine.

'I don't really drink. I'm not worth anything the day after.'

'Well, you're coming out with us.' Sabine turned to Clarissa. 'Where are you taking us?'

'Macleod is taking us out to the most expensive restaurant I can find.'

'And then what?'

'Whatever you spring chickens do,' said Clarissa. 'I want to get back up the road. Frank's missed me. That's a good thing. You don't get a cuddle that good if he hasn't missed you.'

'What about you, Patterson?' said Sabine.

'I'm going in the car of death back up the road,' said Patterson and received a punch in the back from Clarissa. 'Ow,' he said. 'Anyway, as the boss is on the champers, I know who's driving.'

'I am,' said Clarissa. 'But we're not setting off for a couple of hours, so I can have one of these. There's no way I'm missing out on the champers when Macleod's bought it.' The team laughed. 'But we'll have our meal first before we drive up. What are you two going to do? I mean, you're at home, aren't you? What time's a good time out in Glasgow.'

'I haven't really been out in a while. I was thinking about going to the gym. Work off a bit of the tension.'

'I was thinking of settling down to a game at home,' said Emmett.

'A game?'

'Got a new board game arrived today,' said Emmett. 'Want to try it out.'

'Make you a deal,' said Sabine. 'You hit the gym with me. I'll hit the board game with you.'

'Deal,' said Emmett.

Clarissa stood and looked at the pair of them. The Glasgow office was very different. The Inverness office would have been out that night and you wouldn't have seen them the next morning. She'd done karaoke with Macleod, danced the night away. She'd had how many curries? And here, the Glasgow office were off to keep fit, followed by a board game.

It was some four hours later when the little green sports car was making its way back up the A9 towards Inverness. Patterson was asleep in the seat beside Clarissa. There was some old-time music playing, a big band and she was smiling as she drove along. The top was down although it was heading towards night and she wondered if Patterson wouldn't wake up soon, feeling the chill.

Frank had spoken to Clarissa before, saying she didn't need to do this. She'd got lucky this time. A gun to her head. She'd almost been dead. Instead, she turned it around, and they got MacPhail. He'd probably be out in a couple of years. This was artwork they'd grabbed him on. A bit of kidnapping. With his lawyers, who knew what would come. She hoped for a lot more, but she'd seen too many times when things hadn't gone to plan.

She looked across at Patterson. Pats was doing good. He got to question her. He got to give her jibes. No one else did. But he was part of her team. So was Sabine. Sabine, that tall, dynamic style, but she knew her art.

And Emmett—she didn't really know if Emmett fitted on her team, but he'd done well. A strange man, hard not to like, but difficult to love.

She missed the parties though. The big shindigs afterwards, but she'd be home tonight and Frank would have the bath on. Frank and she would sit and watch something, an old movie maybe, and they'd cuddle up. They could do that every night, she thought, but it's not the same when you have done nothing beforehand. The tension. The drama. It was all behind her now. And there was just Frank.

* * *

'So where do I move this piece?' asked Sabine.

'You move it where you want,' said Emmett. 'At the end of the day, it's your choice.'

'I'm still a little confused,' said Sabine. 'These people over here.'

'The Volgons,' said Emmett.

'Yeah, them. Why am I attacking them? I thought they were on my side.'

'No, that's all changed,' said Emmett. 'That changed three rounds ago. They were neutral and now they're against you.'

'Because?' asked Sabine.

'It's in the rules. When you threw a six, it changed.'

Sabine looked down. There was a six-sided die there. But there was also a twenty-sided die. A ten-sided die. A four-sided die. The eight-sided die too.

'Why do we need all these dice?'

Emmett launched into a discussion about the rules. He started telling her about the gameplay, what he thought was good and what he thought was bad. Every now and again, he would aimlessly smile at her.

Sabine just found him wholesome. She sat on the other side of the table, wondering if she'd really found a friend. Were the board games grabbing her? Probably not. But this rather funny little man, who had saved the life of her boss, was warming on her.

Emmett looked up at her. 'I think this is a bit too complicated for you. Maybe we should go for one of the more simple card games.'

'What were you thinking?' asked Sabine.

'Snap,' said Emmett. He ducked as she threw the dice at him.

Read on to discover the Patrick Smythe series!

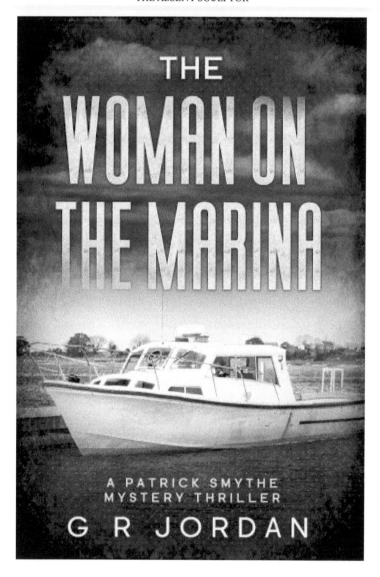

THE
WOMAN ON
THE MARINA

A PATRICK SMYTHE
MYSTERY THRILLER

G R JORDAN

Patrick Smythe is a former Northern Irish policeman who after suffering an amputation after a bomb blast, takes to the sea between the west coast of Scotland and his homeland to ply his trade as a private investigator. Join Paddy as he tries to work to his own ethics while knowing how to bend the rules he once enforced. Working from his beloved motorboat 'Craigantlet', Paddy decides to rescue a drug mule in this short story from the pen of G R Jordan.

Join G R Jordan's monthly newsletter about forthcoming releases and special writings for his tribe of avid readers and then receive your free Patrick Smythe short story.

Go to https://bit.ly/PatrickSmythe for your Patrick Smythe journey to start!

About the Author

GR Jordan is a self-published author who finally decided at forty that in order to have an enjoyable lifestyle, his creative beast within would have to be unleashed. His books mirror that conflict in life where acts of decency contend with self-promotion, goodness stares in horror at evil, and kindness blindsides us when we at our worst. Corrupting our world with his parade of wondrous and horrific characters, he highlights everyday tensions with fresh eyes whilst taking his methodical, intelligent mainstays on a roller-coaster ride of dilemmas, all the while suffering the banter of their provocative sidekicks.

A graduate of Loughborough University where he masqueraded as a chemical engineer but ultimately played American football, Gary had worked at changing the shape of cereal flakes and pulled a pallet truck for a living. Watching vegetables freeze at -40'C was another career highlight and he was also one of the Scottish Highlands "blind" air traffic controllers.

These days he has graduated to answering a telephone to people in trouble before telephoning other people to sort it out.

Having flirted with most places in the UK, he is now based in the Isle of Lewis in Scotland where his free time is spent between raising a young family with his wife, writing, figuring out how to work a loom and caring for a small flock of chickens. Luckily, his writing is influenced by his varied work and life experience as the chickens have not been the poetical inspiration he had hoped for!

You can connect with me on:
🌐 https://grjordan.com
📘 https://facebook.com/carpetlessleprechaun

Subscribe to my newsletter:
✉ https://bit.ly/PatrickSmythe

Also by G R Jordan

G R Jordan writes across multiple genres including crime, dark and action adventure fantasy, feel good fantasy, mystery thriller and horror fantasy. Below is a selection of his work. Whilst all books are available across online stores, signed copies are available at his personal shop.

A Trip to Rome (Highlands & Islands Detective Book 37)

https://grjordan.com/product/a-trip-to-rome

A Scottish tourist found dead in the Colosseum. A killer leaving cryptic clues at historical sites. Can DC Susan Cunningham, still adapting to life on crutches, unravel an international mystery before the Eternal City claims another victim?

When a Highland resident is murdered on vacation in Rome, DC Susan Cunningham is thrust into an investigation that spans two countries. Still recovering from the loss of her lower leg, Susan's determination is put to the test as she navigates Rome's ancient streets on crutches. As she collaborates with Italian authorities, she uncovers a sinister plot connecting Scotland's past to Rome's present. With the clock ticking and cultural tensions rising, can Susan overcome her physical challenges to decipher the ancient riddles and catch a killer who turns history into a deadly game?

In the city of seven hills, every step could be her last!

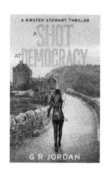

Kirsten Stewart Thrillers
https://grjordan.com/product/a-shot-at-democracy

Join Kirsten Stewart on a shadowy ride through the underbelly of the Highlands of Scotland where among the beauty and splendour of the majestic landscape lies corruption and intrigue to match any city. From murders to extortion, missing children to criminals operating above the law, the Highland former detective must learn a tougher edge to her work as she puts her own life on the line to protect those who cannot defend themselves.

Having left her beloved murder investigation team far behind, Kirsten has to battle personal tragedy and loss while adapting to a whole new way of executing her duties where your mistakes are your own. As Kirsten comes to terms with working with the new team, she often operates as the groups solo field agent, placing herself in danger and trouble to rescue those caught on the dark side of life. With action packed scenes and tense scenarios of murder and greed, the Kirsten Stewart thrillers will have you turning page after page to see your favourite Scottish lass home!

There's life after Macleod, but a whole new world of death!

Jac's Revenge (A Jack Moonshine Thriller #1)
https://grjordan.com/product/jacs-revenge
An unexpected hit makes Debbie a widow. The attention of her man's killer spawns a brutal yet classy alter ego. But how far can you play the game before it takes over your life?

All her life, Debbie Parlor lived in her man's shadow, knowing his work was never truly honest. She turned her head from news stories and rumours. But when he was disposed of for his smile to placate a rival crime lord, Jac Moonshine was born. And when Debbie is paid compensation for her loss like her car was written off, Jac decides that enough is enough.

Get on board with this tongue-in-cheek revenge thriller that will make you question how far you would go to avenge a loved one, and how much you would enjoy it!

A Giant Killing (Siobhan Duffy Mysteries #1)
https://grjordan.com/product/a-giant-killing
A body lies on the Giant's boot. Discord, as the master of secrets has been found. Can former spy Siobhan Duffy find the killer before they execute her former colleagues?

When retired operative Siobhan Duffy sees the killing of her former master in the paper, her unease sends her down a path of discovery and fear. Aided by her young housekeeper and scruff of a gardener, Siobhan begins a quest to discover the reason for her spy boss' death and unravels a can of worms today's masters would rather keep closed. But in a world of secrets, the difference between revenge and simple, if brutal, housekeeping becomes the hardest truth to know.

The past is a child who never leaves home!